Degrees of Evil

John Sturgeon

ISBN: 978-1-61296-901-5
PUBLISHED BY BLACK ROSE WRITING
www.blackrosewriting.com

Printed in the United States of America
Suggested Retail Price (SRP) $18.95

Degrees of Evil is printed in Palatino Linotype
Author Photo courtesy of Mary Sturgeon

"There is really never any good.
There are only different degrees of evil."
~Detective Wilfred Mannus,
New York City Police Department, August 1906

Degrees of Evil

When I kill him, I can only hope that it happens as depicted in the dream. In the dream, I see Christian Hanson many times. I chase him down alleys, into dark parks, passed deserted docks, but I can never catch him. I see him glancing at me, smiling. I can hear him laughing as I give pursuit, but there is always that feeling that my search is in vain. Then there are images of my mother. I have never actually seen her, but she is there. I know it. She has long, dark hair and a clear face. She also smiles, but then she is gone.

It is late at night when I finally corner Hanson on the banks of the Hudson. He is hovering over a female body. I can't make her out. Hanson raises his head to look at me. He smiles. There is blood on his lips and dripping from his teeth, like the Dracula character. The woman, is she dead? Has Hanson fed on her blood or worse? I approach and he stands. He begins to laugh.

I draw my gun and he is now roaring with laughter. The man, who I know cannot speak, now talks. "Too late again, Moses." He rears his head back and the laughter resounds in the empty night air. I aim the revolver and fire.

What I see is his entire heart bursting out of his back. It flies several feet, dripping, and disappears. I look at Hanson. He's still smiling, but then he topples backwards into the cold waters of the Hudson. I walk to the edge of the pier and look over. There is no sight of the body in the murky waters. I walk back to check on the woman, but there is no one there. And then I awake.

I have been in New York for a little over seven months. I have not had a drop of alcohol or a taste of opium. I have set up my office on Forty-Third Street and hired an older woman, Myrtle Robinson, to handle the office when I am not there. I am finding work easily. New York has no lack of infidelity to keep a private detective busy.

I don't miss the Levee. I don't miss the murder, the whores or my favorite crooks, the aldermen. New York has all of that, so what is there to miss? What New York has is my mother, if she is still alive, and Christian Hanson. Other than my dream, I have not seen either one of them. If they are here I will find them. I'm a detective. That is what I do.

*****

August 3, 1906

Myrtle Robinson appears in my office doorway. Once in her life, I can see, she was quite attractive, but that was years ago. Now, she is older and wears the dresses of a retired school teacher, which is what she is. She always gives me the look that tells me that she is watching or maybe keeping an eye on me. I don't mind.

"There is a cop here to see you," she says.

I raise my eyes from the morning paper. "How do you know he is a cop?"

"He has that same look that you have, the one that says you don't trust anyone. That and he told me he was a cop."

Since my move to middle Manhattan, I have formed a friendly bond with the local precinct. At first they checked me out, the new private eye in their realm. Things must have come back okay because they leave me alone and occasionally will throw a bone my way.

"Do you want me to show him in?" Myrtle asks.

"Sure," I said. "Why not?"

The cop is a detective, Wilfred Mannus. He is tall, almost six and half feet and his width fills my doorway as he squeezes past Myrtle. His hands are a big as a catcher's mitt. They easily engulf mine when we shake. Size is one thing. Mannus has soft, blonde hair, blue eyes and no signs of any beard or mustache growth. He looks sixteen.

"So you came here from Chicago," he says. The voice is smooth, not making him sound older.

"Almost eight months."

"Much difference in what you see?"

How to phrase this answer? "I came from a Hell Hole on earth. The Levee District. I've heard you have some areas that may match it, but I haven't seen them yet. Not that I'm looking."

Mannus nodded and lit a cigarette. I pushed an ashtray in his direction. "Can't say I blame you," he said, exhaling a large plume of smoke towards the ceiling. "What I have for you today won't involve anything like that. In fact, we're dealing with something from the Upper East Side."

I knew the area, mostly highbrow types. Money. Much like my old friends from Prairie Avenue in Chicago. "Something stolen?"

"Yes, you could say that. The three children of Flynn and Rebecca Colton. They were taken from a babysitter's yard about a week ago. No one has seen them or heard a word from anyone about them. Highly unusual in kidnappings."

I watched Mannus inhale half the cigarette, the red end glowing brightly. "This sounds like a police matter."

"It clearly is, Mr. Moses, but if I must be honest with you, we are clearly stumped. We have no clues, no suspects. The children were playing in the yard of the babysitter one minute and gone the next. No one heard or saw anything. That status has not changed since they were taken."

"And what do you think I can do for you?"

"Me?" he said, laughing. "We have the whole damn force looking for these kids. These are good cops. They have found nothing. I don't really think you'll be able to do much better."

"Someone in your department must think otherwise."

"You are correct, Moses. Word has gotten to the department that right in our midst we have the Great Detective, Patrick Moses, the man responsible for cracking the Hobbs' kidnapping in Chicago earlier this year. Someone with much more authority than me has asked if you would be willing to give us a hand."

Mannus wasn't giving me that much encouragement. "Who are these Coltons?"

"Flynn is the son of one of the largest shipping magnates in New York. Rebecca is a very good looking woman, who from what I understand, does whatever she wants to."

Now it was my turn to laugh. They sounded more and more like my Prairie Avenue friends. "And the children?"

"Maria, seven, Constance, five and Flynn Junior, three."

"I get my normal fees and expenses?"

"That and I have been told that as a private citizen, you would be in line for the reward the Coltons have posted. It is a hundred thousand dollars."

"Where do I sign up?" I said.

• • •

We rode in a police van that Mannus had waiting for us outside of my office. The day was hot and I could feel the humidity in the air; my shirt was already starting to stick to my back. I hoped the ride to the Upper East Side wouldn't take that long.

"I hear you are looking for a blonde man who parts his hair down the middle," Mannus said. "He also doesn't talk."

I had mentioned Hanson to some of the boys at the local precinct. They had obviously told Mannus of my quest. "He is also a crazy bastard, but that is true. His name is Christian Hanson. He has killed a couple of friends of mine, detectives, along with several others."

Mannus flicked the last of his cigarette out of the carriage. "There was a saloonkeeper over in the Five Points who was shot and robbed. A witness saw a blonde man, hair parted down the middle, running from the bar to a waiting carriage. Another person told us this same man had been in the bar before, said he couldn't speak. We think he might be muscle for the Black Hand, a gang that controls a lot of territory in Manhattan."

"That sounds like him and that would be his specialty. The Five Points, you say?"

"A tough area. If you plan on going down there, let me know. It might not be wise for an out of towner to go poking around. The natives may get a little restless."

I nodded quietly and took my hat off to wipe my moist brow. "So these Coltons. What can you tell me about them other than they are rich?"

Mannus laughed. "They are definitely rich. The husband is a bit of a spoiled child. Wasn't told no very much in his life. From what I can gather, he works hard and plays hard. Likes good scotch and doesn't seem to mind the ladies."

"But he's married," I said.

"They told us you were a good detective, not that you'd done vaudeville. Mr. Colton has been known to keep a mistress or two. Apparently his father has asked him more than once to curtail this behavior, but so far his advice had gone unheeded."

I thought of Marshall Field and his son, both now dead. "And the wife?"

"A nice woman, from what I can gather. Since the kidnapping we haven't been able to really talk with her. She's emotionally run down and has been under sedation. Shock likely."

"Hard to blame her. Do they employ staff?"

"Of course. A full time maid and chef, both had the day off the day of the kidnapping. There is also Mr. Colton's valet, a huge Negro by the name of Custis. He drives Colton in his carriage and acts as his bodyguard. We were told he's been with the family since Lincoln ended slavery. He was taken in when he was ten. He's more loyal to Colton than most dogs and maybe more dangerous."

"Where was Custis the day of the crime?"

"With Colton all day."

"How about the babysitter?"

"A lovely, middle-aged woman, Mrs. Marsh. She watches the children each Tuesday while Mrs. Colton runs errands and shops. She had left the children in the small yard in the rear of her home. This was a common practice of hers. She was in the house for a few minutes, she says, not much more. When she came back out, the children were gone. She, as you might imagine, is totally distraught."

"I can imagine. Married, Mannus?"

"Call me Will. I am and we have a little girl, Claire."

I could see him thinking about little Claire, about how he would feel if some son of a bitch took her. "I have seen a lot of people who have had loved ones murdered. Usually, there's a reason for the crime and people grieve for a bit and then, sadly, life goes on. With little children it's a bit different. No one ever understands why anyone would want to hurt a little kid. Regardless of the outcome of the case, they will never understand."

Mannus nodded. "I think you should know that the Colton family, more the business, has garnered a number of enemies over the years. I gather that some of their business dealings have been contentious. When I asked Colton about this, he only laughed. He told me it would take weeks for him to come up with a list of people that either his father or he had angered over the years."

The carriage had pulled up to an impressive, three story brownstone on Sixty- Eighth Street. "He may laugh and think it's funny, but if it takes him weeks to give us information that we need, his children might end up dead."

Mannus grimaced. "The same thought crossed my mind."

Before we walked up the stairs to the brownstone, I couldn't help but think of the similarities between the Coltons and the Hobbs. Rich people, big homes, chefs, maids and missing children. The Hobbs' twins had been snatched from their bedroom; the Colton's from a sitter's yard. One more thing that I was certain of. All of those children would be scared.

The maid, a Ms. Cobb, a young Negro woman, answered the door almost immediately. She was a petite thing, a bit chubby with high cheek bones. She led us into the sitting room which faced the street. Mannus sat in a large stuffed chair. I remained standing. The room was lined with bookshelves and smelled of cigars. There was also the head of an enormous elk posted over the fireplace. It didn't look very happy.

"A hunter in the family?"

Mannus shrugged. "Money allows you to hunt different things than what you and I are usually after."

"Most things we are after have only two legs."

"Animals nonetheless."

"Touché'" I answered.

"Gentlemen, I am sorry to have kept you waiting." Through the door that we had just entered came a tall man, broad shouldered, big necked with hair as dark as a crow and a thick bushy mustache. He was wearing an expensive Sailor and Sons suit, where all of the buttons had a little anchor on them. He approached us in log strides. "I am Flynn Colton."

Colton shook my hand firmly as I was already standing. He looked hard at me with two deep blue eyes and then proceeded to shake Mannus' hand. Behind him, standing just inside the doorway, stood a large black man, completely bald. As tall and wide as Colton was, his valet dwarfed him. His eyes were staring straight ahead, appearing not to see, but seeing everything.

"Mr. Colton, this is Detective Patrick Moses, from the Chicago Police Department."

"The solver of the Hobbs Elevator kidnapping," Colton said.

"Nobody kidnapped an elevator, Mr. Colton. They were twin babies, eighteen month old," I said.

Colton smiled. "Yes, of course. I meant no disrespect at what I said."

"Detective Moses has been asked to help us out," Mannus said. His look towards me implored me to behave.

"We are glad to have your help, Detective. Now, where do we get started?"

"Will your wife be joining us for these discussions?" I asked.

"Currently, Rebecca is resting. Doctor's orders. She has been administered a sedative to help her sleep."

"Eventually we will need to speak with her."

"I understand, Detective. Now, as I have said, is not the time."

I nodded. "So, Mr. Colton, what can you tell us about the day that your children disappeared?"

Colton looked over at Mannus. "I have already relayed this information to the police. I believe they probably have it recorded somewhere."

"I'm sure they do," I said. "I'd like you to tell me, unless there is a more convenient time."

I heard Mannus grunt as Colton scrunched his mustache and seemed like he might want to strangle me. "Where would you like me to start?"

"From the start of that day. Maybe telling the story again will reveal something different. I know this is tough, but it all may help."

"Well, I leave for my office each day around seven. My schedule has been a little different since the kids were taken. We're located on Lexington near Tenth Street. On Tuesdays Rebecca leaves the children with Mrs. Marsh. She usually drops them right before lunch and then takes a carriage into Mid-town to run errands and do a little shopping. Since it is summer, all three children would have been dropped off.

"From what we understand, around three o'clock Mrs. Marsh stepped into her house to fix the children some lemonade. It was hot that day, like today. She left the kids in a little side yard. She was in the house approximately seven to ten minutes. When she returned to the yard the kids were gone. There is a gate on the side of the yard facing the street. It was closed and latched. Obviously, she panicked and started walking around the house, shouting for the children. She pounded on a few neighbor's doors. Nothing had been heard or seen. She went back into her house and called the police and then she called my office. I was out on the docks by then and didn't get the message until later. Naturally, I raced home to Rebecca."

"And your wife. When did she hear about the kidnapping?"

"Only when she returned to Mrs. Marsh's house to retrieve the children. That was between five and five-thirty. Then, for the first time, she heard the news. She immediately felt weak and a doctor was called. She was then taken back to our house, arriving about the time I got the message at my office."

"And that is all you know?"

"At this time yes. The police can tell you what they know, of course, but we have no other knowledge. Because of who we are I expected a quick ransom demand, but have heard nothing. Someone has taken my three children, but it's more like they have vanished. That is what scares me the most, not hearing anything."

"That is a bit unusual," I said, referring to the ransom. "I understand both the maid and the chef have Tuesday off."

"They do."

"I'll have to speak with them privately and I will need to speak with your wife when she is feeling better, which I hope is soon."

"Of course," Colton said. "Do you want to speak with the staff now? They are both here."

"Not now. Now, I think it would be advisable to speak with Mrs. Marsh to see what she knows. Someone of familiarity took your children, Mr. Colton. They were taken in broad daylight without a scuffle or a noise being made. I think someone who knew them quite well is the person we are looking for."

Colton look shocked at this news. He politely shook our hands and showed us to the front door. As we passed the large man, Custis, his eyes never moved. He was a formidable figure. A scary one at that.

• • • •

Mrs. Marsh looked like everyone's mother. She was a short, portly woman dressed in a well-worn house dress. Unfortunately the whole time we met with her she sat on a couch in her front room, sniffling and blowing her nose into a soaked handkerchief. From what we could gather, she had been in this spot, since the theft of the children. The crime had rocked her constitution.

"In the summer months, Maria, the oldest girl comes to my home as well," she said. "She is a very bright girl, a good girl. I could trust her to keep any eye on the little ones for a minute when I went into the house. That day, like every other day that they came over, I told Maria I was going into the house to make lemonade. I told her to keep an eye on the other two kids until I returned. Like always she said to me, 'Yes, Mrs. Marsh', and I knew she would keep an eye on them. I was in the house no more than ten minutes. When I returned, they were all gone." This dialogue brought forth another barrage of tears and we had to wait for her to get under control before we could continue.

"You didn't hear or see anything that day that was amiss?" I asked.

She shook her head. "Nothing. I heard nothing. I saw nothing. I came back and they were gone."

"Can we see the yard that the kids were taken from?" I asked.

The yard area was small. It was completely surrounded by a short iron fence with a gate on the street side. Along the fence grew a vast number of colorful flowers, all now fully in bloom. In the center of the yard was a grassy area where the children played.

"It's not a very large area," Mannus said.

"I know, Detective," Mrs. Marsh answered, "but it is enough to allow the children to get out and play a bit, to get some fresh air."

I looked back at the house. Only one small window and a door looked out on the yard. "You can't see the yard from the kitchen?" I asked.

She saw what I was looking at. "No, just from the door if it's open or from that window. That's a small storage room. The kitchen is to the right of the door as you enter it. Its' windows face the other side of the house."

There really wasn't much more to ask or see. The children were in the yard playing when Mrs. Marsh went in to make the lemonade. When she came back the children were gone. It still seemed to me that someone who knew the children, someone that they would be comfortable with, came by and took them.

"Is there a Mr. Marsh?" I asked.

"There is," she said.

"Where was he when the children were taken?"

Her face tensed with obvious worry at the question. "He is a brick layer, laid off. I'm pretty sure he was at the hall trying to find work."

Mannus nodded. "That should do it for now."

• • •

In the carriage, on the way back to mid-town, Mannus lit another cigarette. "You seem pretty certain that the kidnapper has to be someone that the children knew."

I thought for a moment. "I don't know about certain, but that is my first thought. Here it is the middle of the day. Three children out in a yard, playing. If they had been forcibly abducted you would think there would have been some noise, maybe one of the kids crying out, but there is nothing. My first thought was that someone who knew the children showed up with a mode of transportation and they got into it and left."

Mannus puffed nervously at the smoke, his eyes wandering the compartment. "Well, we've got the parents, the two employees who were off that day and now Herbert Marsh. We didn't ask about him before."

I liked the way he was thinking. "His motive would be?"

"An out of work bricklayer, his wife said. His motive, of course, is money."

"But seven days later, no request for ransom. Not a peep for anything."

"So he's not a suspect?"

"Maybe, maybe not. Same goes for the employees. They could be behind it, but their motive would be the same, money. The length of time from the crime until today is getting close to excluding anyone who was looking for cash. Where do you quietly hide three young children for a week? Somebody would see or hear something, unless the children knew the kidnapper and were quiet."

"So we're down to the people who money is not a factor?"

"Or someone we don't know about, but again, if it's money then how come we haven't heard anything?"

"What about just pure evil?"

I thought of how Colton had talked about the number of enemies his business had built up. Sweat ran down my back and I shivered. "I know a little about evil and there is always evil. Let's hope and pray that is not the case."

Mannus' eyes narrowed. "There is always evil. It just comes at us in different degrees. What did you think of Colton?"

"A little smug, arrogant. The typical rich type. They believe that the world hangs on their last word. Several of my last cases in Chicago had me dealing with this type. I know it well."

"You don't seemed thrilled with the wealthy."

"Rich people feel they are entitled to things that we are not. Because of this there is a large number of problems that arise that are not normal to the investigation. This has caused me a certain bias against the affluent."

"Did he seem a bit casual to you? Maybe a bit uncaring?"

I shrugged. "Maybe a little, but I think most things that these types don't plan come across as an inconvenience. I'm sure his children's kidnapping is a tremendous inconvenience for Mr. Colton."

*****

August 4th

I have slept better since I moved to New York. I'm sure this has a lot to do with quitting the booze and the opium, but in the Levee District you are constantly surrounded by bad. I thought of what Mannus said about evil. It was always in the Levee, but I hadn't really come in contact with it in Manhattan. I had been sleeping well, except for last night.

"You don't look well, Mr. Moses," Myrtle Robinson said. She was standing in my doorway looking at me like I had done something wrong.

"I didn't sleep as well as I would have liked."

Another scornful look. "You didn't find a whiskey bottle, did you?"

I had told her of some of my problems in Chicago. "No whiskey, or gin or vodka. Just bad sleep."

"Well, you might want to feel a little better. You have a visitor."

"Someone important, I hope."

"I think so. It is Flynn Colton's mother."

Suzanne Colton was somewhere north of fifty, a smart looking woman who carried herself in a professional manner. The suit she wore was expensive and well-tailored. Her hair and make-up were both professionally done. When she shook my hand I could tell the polish on her nails was not cheap, like most of the ladies in the Levee. I liked her right away, including the brash manner that she conducted business.

"I have been told that you have taken over the investigation of my grandchildren's kidnapping." She sat across from me, legs crossed, looking like she didn't want to hear any bullshit.

"That is not accurate. I am merely assisting the New York police."

"Fair enough. Flynn was the one who told me you seemed like you might be in charge."

I wanted to say I'd never been in charge of anything, but didn't. "I have been retained to help find the children."

"And what have you found so far?"

Taken aback, I didn't answer right away. "Mrs. Colton, you are aware that I was hired only yesterday?"

"Yes, almost twenty-four hours. You must have learned something."

"That is true. I learned that the kids were in the yard of Mrs. Marsh one minute and the next minute they were gone. No one heard or saw anything. This leads me to believe they were taken by someone who the children knew. Now, a week later, there has been no request for ransom or word about the children. This is very odd, especially if the motive for the kidnapping is money."

She laughed out loud and I stopped talking. "The person who took these three children didn't do it for money. They did it for attention."

"Attention?" I stuttered. "You're implying that you know who took them?"

"I do, Detective Moses. My daughter-in-law, Rebecca, took the children."

Where I had felt a little groggy prior to her arrival, I was suddenly wide awake. "That is a rather strong accusation. What makes you think that your daughter-in-law had anything to do with the kidnapping?"

"Her jealousy, of course."

"Her jealousy got her to commit this crime? What is she jealous of?"

She frowned at me. "Rebecca is jealous of Flynn. Where Flynn has something to do all day long, she has nothing. That girl requires complete attention, one hundred percent of the time. She is also convinced that my son is wandering around with several mistresses. Between Flynn being very busy and her fantasy of him having a lover, she did this to draw attention to herself."

I didn't want to bring up what Mannus told me about Flynn Colton's alleged romancing. "Let me make sure that I understand you correctly. You think Rebecca took the children to get her husband's attention?"

"That is it exactly."

"So where are the children now?"

She smiled. "We are a wealthy family, Detective Moses. There are a number of places I'm sure she could have taken them to where they are being treated perfectly and fed quite well."

"All for attention?"

"You met the maid, Ms. Cobb?"

"I did."

"She has told me repeatedly that Rebecca complains constantly about the hours Flynn has to keep and that she says they never spend any time together. She has claimed more than once that Flynn loves his work much more than he loves her."

"A common malady, I hear," but this comment got nothing more than a dead stare from her. "What do you suggest I do?"

"You're the detective, aren't you? I suggest you get over there and question her."

"The last I heard, yesterday, was that she wasn't feeling well and was sedated."

"Well, I left there to come here. Flynn and Rebecca are both awake and well. The whole staff is present. I think now would be a good time to get over there and talk to her."

I found myself stupidly nodding, but we were soon in Suzanne Colton's carriage on the way uptown to the Colton residence.

• • •

As I stepped out of the carriage, I could tell that it was going to be another oppressively hot day. It was not quite ten o'clock and the air was thick with humidity. The thought of absurd requests from rich people crossed my mind. I had seen it before, but what did I have to lose from this little visit? We had nothing.

"Back so soon," Flynn Colton said confidently, rising from a chair in the dining room.

There was a small woman seated to his side. She looked tired and like she had just risen from bed. She wore no makeup and her hair could use a brush stroke or two.

"I'm surprised to see you here," I said. "Yesterday, you said you were usually out the door by seven."

He shook my hand, but not with the vigor of the day before. "Rebecca finally made it out of bed and I wanted to spend some time with her."

"But you always go into the office, even since the kidnapping?"

He smiled weakly. "It helps me keep my sanity."

I nodded and stepped around Colton and offered Rebecca Colton my hand. She shook it weakly and stared up at me with eyes that were red, puffy and raw looking. Cried out, I would say. "Mrs. Colton," I said.

It was then that I noticed the black valet, Custis, standing near the corner in the shadows of the room. I wanted to think that he nodded at me, but I wasn't sure.

"You didn't answer my question," Colton said. "Why are you back so soon? Have you found something?"

This question caused Rebecca to look up quickly. "Nothing like that," I said.

"I told Detective Moses that everyone, including Rebecca, were at the house and now might be a good time to talk with them," Suzanne Colton said from behind me.

Flynn gave her an admonishing look. "Really, mother? A good time."

"I'm fine," the small voice of Rebecca Colton said. "Detective Moses has come all the way here. The least I can do is answer a few questions."

Suzanne was smiling at her son; he wasn't very pleased.

"Would it be okay if I questioned Mrs. Colton privately?" I asked.

Colton's arms came up quickly and he crossed them over his chest. "Is that necessary?"

"That's fine, Flynn," Rebecca said. "We'll be right here in this room. I don't think anything bad will happen, will it, Detective?"

I smiled at her. "I doubt it very much."

"Leave us for a bit," Rebecca said. "There's so little I know or can say, this shouldn't take that long."

The other three cleared the room and I was alone with Rebecca. If I had one word to describe her it would be frail. A once pretty woman had been shrunken down to a faded picture of her future. I knew she wasn't that old, but she looked old and worn out. There didn't appear to be any color in her face. The kidnapping had taken away a good part of her life. If she was responsible at all, she was doing an excellent job of masking her involvement.

She took a sip of her tea. "Sit down, Detective," she said. "I'm ready whenever you are."

I took the seat right next to her where Flynn had been sitting. He had left a full plate of food. His wife was only getting by on tea. "Are you feeling okay, Mrs. Colton? I know that is a stupid question, but I am concerned."

She smiled weakly. "Thank you, Detective. I haven't slept very much in the past week, but I suppose I'm doing about as well as can be expected."

I didn't know what to respond if anything; I shifted uneasily on the chair.

"I've had this dream several times since the children were taken from us. It's the same dream. The kids are all lying is a dark place. I can see they are not moving. I can see they are not breathing. Their eyes are completely shut."

"That's just a bad dream," I said.

She smiled weakly. "I hear you are an expert on kidnappings."

I had worked one kidnapping in my life and solved it. Did that make me an expert? "I have had experience with kidnappings?"

"My children are dead, aren't they?"

Her face was staring at me; there was no emotion in the voice. I think all emotion had drained from her. "We have no way of knowing anything definitive about the children."

She placed her hand over mine. To the touch hers was cold. "A week has gone by. There has been no ransom demand. There hasn't been any word at all. You don't have to try and soften me up. Whoever took them has killed them and when he killed them he killed me. I will never be able to go on as before, to live any kind of normal life. Their death was my death."

I was a little spooked. This was either legitimate or maybe she had done something to the children to draw sympathy from others and was now giving the acting performance of her life.

"Don't you want to ask me questions about that day? Isn't that what you're supposed to do?"

"Not that day, but Tuesdays in general. Tell me what you usually do on Tuesdays."

"That is the one day that I give myself a little time off. You see, we have a maid and a chef, but we have no nanny. I take the children as my responsibility. I spend all the time with them that I can, but not on Tuesday. Once we have our breakfast and we get ready for the day I drop them off at Mrs. Marsh's for the afternoon. Then I go downtown or into Mid-town for some shopping. Most of the time I leave them for a couple of hours. Sometimes I'm gone until about five, but no later than that."

"You were gone until five on the day of the kidnapping."

"I was. I got to looking at dresses, trying on a few. Time went by much more quickly than I thought."

"So you have followed this Tuesday pattern for some time?"

She nodded and slowly sipped her tea. "Since Maria was about two, so maybe five years. I would take a little break when one of the children was a newborn, but not very long. Mrs. Marsh is very good with children, even babies."

"And you trust her?"

"Absolutely. I wouldn't leave my children with her if I didn't."

"Have you ever met her husband?"

She thought for a moment. "I wouldn't say met. I have seen him and exchanged pleasantries, but I can't say I've actually spoken much to him."

"What about the practice of leaving the children in the yard while Mrs. Marsh went into the house to get lemonade?"

"My oldest daughter, Maria, told us about it. Mrs. Marsh would go into the house and get the drinks and cookies for the kids. She would leave Maria in charge, telling her to come right away if there was any kind of a problem."

"Did Maria ever tell you anything strange about the days at Mrs.

Marsh's? Did she ever see anyone that scared her, especially while out in the yard? She ever say anything about anyone talking to her?"

"Never."

I thought for a moment. A rather common practice of leaving the children to fix lemonade and get cookies. Something that the oldest daughter had told her mother about.

"Let me change the topic a bit and if it appears that I'm getting out of line, I apologize, but you must know that everyone is a suspect until they are cleared."

Her eyes tightened, but she said nothing.

"Have things been okay between you and Mr. Colton?"

She smiled. "We have been married over ten years, Detective. Do you know anyone married that long where everything is perfect?"

"I suppose not," I said.

"We have our good moments and our bad," she continued. "Flynn works very long hours and sometimes he doesn't get home until late and the children are already asleep. This also doesn't allow much time for us to be alone."

"Again, I apologize, but I've heard rumors that you think Flynn might be involved with another woman, causing stress to your own relationship."

She stared for a moment. "What does this have to do with the kidnapping?"

"I'd like to know all of the people involved at the time of the crime. Anyone out there who can gain from the children being taken, whoever that might be."

"Flynn is a good looking man and is extremely wealthy. He goes to a lot of functions. There are usually women at these functions. I would highly doubt that none of them have never advanced themselves at my husband."

"But you know of no single woman who he might be involved with?"

"I don't," she said flatly. "He is home every night in my bed. It is not the perfect marriage, but it is not the worst."

I sighed. "Mrs. Colton, who do you think kidnapped your children?"

She sipped her tea and thought on that for a second. "Someone evil. Someone with hate in their soul. If they wanted money we'd have heard a demand by now. This was done with pure malice as the intent."

There was Mannus' word evil again. "But no names of anyone?"

Now she laughed. "Only one of the hundred or so people that Flynn or his father have ruined or tried to ruin through their business."

Again the business and the number of people it ruined. I thanked her and left her to her tea.

• • • • •

I found the maid, Mary Cobb, in one of the rear rooms. She was busy dusting and didn't hear me enter the room. I cleared my throat loudly and she turned to see me in the doorway.

"I'm sorry, Detective. I didn't hear you there," she said. She dropped the duster that she was using on the cabinets and stood up straight to face me.

"I didn't mean to interrupt your work."

She smiled weakly. "It's only dusting." She was an attractive girl with a light brown colored skin.

"I'd like to ask you a few questions if you don't mind."

"Do I have a choice?"

Now it was my turn to smile. "I guess I could have you arrested if you don't cooperate."

"That doesn't sound very pleasant, so I'll answer whatever I can."

"During your daily duties, did you have a lot of contact with the children?"

"I would see them every day, and they are all sweet little kids, but I didn't have that much to do with them. Mrs. Colton is a devoted mother and spends most of the time with the children. The only day that she is not with them is Tuesday. Of course that's the day they were..."

"Kidnapped."

"Yes, sir."

"Tuesday is also your day off."

"It is. The Tuesday they were taken, like any other Tuesday, I spend with my mother. I live with her in Harlem. She is not well. That is the one day I spend with her."

I nodded. "Very well. Who do you think might have kidnapped the children?"

She paused to think for a bit. "Someone horrible. Who takes three little children? My guess is that is someone who is very upset with Mr. Colton, but I have no way of knowing anything."

"I have heard the Mrs. Colton is very upset about all the time that Mr. Colton spends away from the house, working and whatever."

She smiled again. She had perfect white teeth. I liked her. "He does work a lot. As for the whatever, you hear a lot of things, but again, I don't know anything. I also would prefer to keep this position."

"Whatever you say stays between us. Do you think Mrs. Colton would ever do anything to those children to draw attention to herself?"

"Now I see where you're going. Mrs. Colton has complained to me privately about all of the time that Mr. Colton spends away from the house. I have also heard separate rumors that Mr. Colton keeps a mistress or two. I'm sure Mrs. Colton has heard the same stories. I would say Mrs. Colton is not that happy with the current state of their marriage; I would say she craves more attention, but I don't think she would ever do anything to hurt those kids, even if it meant drawing attention to herself. Look at her. This has taken the life out of her. You can't fake how she looks and feels .She looks like she is on the verge of a breakdown."

"Unless you are a great actor," I said without thinking.

"She is not acting, sir."

I nodded again. "What of the cook, Mr. Benson?"

"Luther? I can tell you without a doubt that Mr. Benson works every Tuesday, his day off, at the First Baptist Church in Harlem. I will bet you that he was there from dawn until night fall."

"What of Custis?"

Now the look was stern. "What of him?"

"Everybody has a story."

"His parents were slaves over in Virginia. Once the war ended Mr. Colton's father took him in to help. I think he was about ten. He has been with the family ever since. When Mr. Colton returned from college, Custis was assigned to him as a valet."

"He doesn't talk much."

"Not to white people."

"That's understandable. Will he talk to me?"

"You look pretty white."

"I guess I'm asking a favor."

Again that smile and those white teeth. "I can ask him for you."

"That would be a big help."

She took a couple of steps toward me and her look went quickly to sad. "Do you think the children are okay?"

A week was a long time without hearing anything. It was very odd. "I don't know."

"Please try and find them. If something bad has happened to them, I don't think Mrs. Colton will recover."

• • •

Flynn Colton was standing in the foyer of his house when I returned from my discussion with Mary Cobb; I had heard his mother had left. Again, he was dressed in a Sailor and Sons suit, this time a dark blue. He seemed a little more agitated when he saw me.

"Ah, Detective Moses, I assume your discussions have gone well?"

I didn't know how well they'd gone. I'd learned very little. "I have succeeded at my task, let me say that."

A smug little smile crossed his lips. "And do you think you are any closer to finding my children?"

This I could answer. "I think there are a couple of people out there who I can dismiss as suspects. I also think I am going to need more information."

"What type of information would that be?"

"Everyone that I talk to, without fail, has made mention of the fact that you and your father have made many enemies as you have built your business."

"I'm afraid that is true, but you will probably see that in any line of business where the larger concerns put some of the smaller ones out of business."

"I understand that, but has business always gone about in a professional and ethical manner?"

His smile widened. "That is a tough thing to do, particularly in New York and in the shipping business."

"That's what I mean," I said. "What I am interested in is a list of clients who you have competed with, and maybe defeated, in the past couple of years. I'm really interested in the situations where things got heavily contentious."

His smile was quickly gone. "As I told the police, compiling a list like that could take an enormous amount of time."

"Detective Mannus told me that, but I'm asking you to complete the list. I can't relate to you the importance of it. We are already a week behind. The most logical choice of someone taking your children for pure hate is someone you have upset through business dealings. The fact that no one has come forward suggesting a ransom leads me to think whoever did this did it to get at you."

"Your first thought was that someone who the children knew took them."

"Doesn't mean that someone you upset through a business dealing couldn't have gone in with someone the children know."

His mouth dropped open and there was no smile. "I will try and compile something quickly."

I thanked him and stepped back out into the August heat. It was just past noon and the sun was high in the sky, blocked only by buildings and trees. Even in the shade the heat and humidity were stifling. In the heat, even the nicest parts of this city had certain smells that weren't that pleasant. Just like the Levee.

• • •

Will Mannus was in my office when I returned. Myrtle was not there. Will was sitting in my chair, in my private office, feet on the desk, reading the *New York Times*.

"I hope you are comfortable," I said.

He seemed a little shocked that I had come into the office without him hearing me. His feet came off the desk and he folded the paper and put it back in the center of my desk. "Mrs. Robinson had to step out for a moment," he said. "I was watching the office for her. She didn't know when to expect you back."

I sat in one of the guest chairs across from Mannus. "Anything good in the news?"

"Not really. What got me the most was that the Colton children have been gone eight days. Only eight days. I couldn't find a thing in the paper about their kidnapping."

This was true in Chicago as well. In big cities there was always something going on to make it to the first page. Yesterday's news eventually just disappeared. "I had a very nice conversation with Rebecca Colton. Of course, this was after her mother-in-law tipped me that she was probably the lead suspect."

Mannus sat back and lit a cigarette. "Is she?"

"I hardly think so. The kidnapping, not knowing what happened to her children, is tearing her apart, mentally and physically. She isn't even suspect number ten. According to the maid, if something awful has happened to the children, there is a very good chance that Mrs. Colton may require constant care."

"That bad, huh?"

"She sees the children dead in her dreams and believes they are gone."

Mannus shook his head. "And the maid?"

"A very nice young lady. Home with her sick mother all day the day of the crime. The cook works at a church up in Harlem on his days off. The maid told me she knew he was there that day as well."

"So dead ends are piling up?"

"I would say so at this point. Nothing on your end?"

"We went by the union halls, checking on George Marsh. He hasn't been in looking for work in over a week, but we were tipped off that he spends a lot of his days at Shannon's Tavern near Twelfth Street. That was wear we found him. Apparently he had spent the good part of each day there the last month. I don't think he kidnapped anyone."

"Is it always this hot here in August?"

Mannus shrugged. "It is summer, but it does seem unusually warm and humid."

"The city smells, too."

"You get that in a big city."

"I also saw Flynn Colton and asked him to put together a list of possible business contacts from the past two years that he would consider enemies."

"I'm sure he was thrilled about that."

"Told me the same thing he told your men, that it would take forever. Finally he agreed to do it."

Mannus puffed out a tremendous ring of smoke right over the top of my head. "So, who did it Moses?"

The smoke started to descend upon me and dissipate. "My bet today is someone who hates the Colton family. I'm leaning towards a business deal that got testy. They probably did it in concert with someone the children know."

"That seems logical. What do we do now?"

"That I don't have an answer for good or bad. Let's see who Mr. Colton puts on his list."

Mannus looked depressed at my answer. The front door opened and Myrtle was back from her errand. She poked her head in my office. "I see you two found each other," she said."

"Remind me to not hire you for security," I said.

She didn't smile. "You know this city really smells when it gets this hot."

*****

Chicago

Inside the apartment located on the second floor, the heat had risen to more than one hundred degrees. Even when the two detectives and the criminologist opened all of the windows there wasn't much relief. There wasn't much of a breeze outside and what there was wasn't cooling anything off. The apartment was small with one bedroom, a sitting area, a kitchen and a small bathroom. It was nicely decorated and everything was neat with one exception. The heat wasn't the worst thing about the apartment. The worst thing was the smell from the dead body tied to the chair in the center of the sitting room.

"How long do you think she has been sitting here like this?" George Loftus asked. He was smoking a cigarette as quickly as he could, trying hard to eliminate some of the smell with its smoke.

"Hard to say," Harold Pinter said, "but based on the smell and the amount of rigor mortis, I'd say five to seven days. We may be able to pinpoint a closer time frame once we can talk to some of the other tenants in the building."

Riley O'Donnell stepped forward and looked down at the body. "Is she as old as the first one?"

Pinter looked at him. "Appears to be of a similar age. I'd say late seventies, early eighties."

The body in the chair was the lone resident of the apartment. Her name was Dorothy Casson. The chair she was on was a wooden kitchen type. Her hands were tied behind her back and her ankles were tied to two of the chair's legs. A cut up bed sheet had been used to secure her to the chair. Another piece of sheet had been tied tightly across her eyes. Stuffing from the inside of a pillow had been forced into both ears, her nostrils and her mouth. She had been tied very tightly to the chair, her back very upright. Only her head sagged to her left side.

"What do you think killed her?" Loftus asked.

Pinter laughed. "George, I don't know. This poor old gal could have died from fright, heart failure or suffocation. Hopefully one of those causes took her rather quickly."

"Who does this to old ladies?" Riley asked.

There was no answer from the other two. The group's conversation was interrupted by a knocking at the door. It was opened and Lieutenant Richard Shipley entered the apartment. Shipley had been assigned to run the 22nd Precinct until a replacement could be found. It was almost seven months. No one had been found.

Shipley took a handkerchief out of his pocket to cover his mouth. Loftus and Riley smiled and lowered their heads. "Is it similar to the first murder?" Shipley asked in his high pitched voice.

"I would say exactly," Harold Pinter said. "She is bound in the same fashion and with the same implements."

"Two murders of old women who live by themselves," Shipley said.

"Not just murders," Loftus said. "These women were tortured and then suffocated."

"My goodness," Shipley said.

"This is not really our case, Lieutenant," Riley said.

Shipley gave him a dirty look. "The first murder, Mrs. Muldor, took place in the Levee. There's no doubt the murders are connected. Headquarters wants us to follow it. They also like the fact the Mr. Pinter is involved. George, you and Riley, will head the team, using the local precinct patrolmen to assist you in anything you need."

"What we need is more help. We are up to our necks in cases and don't seem to have enough time to stay current on any of them," George Loftus said.

"I've been putting in ten, twelve hours a day," Riley said.

Shipley nodded. "I have a suggestion."

The other three turned to look at him. "I think there is a possibility that we can get Moses back here to help us."

"Why would he come back here?" Loftus said. "The Levee is no garden spot and this case is not going to be simple or pleasant."

"Mr. Pinter?" Shipley said.

"I cabled him after the first murder for his thoughts. He seemed intrigued and asked a lot of good questions. He also stated that if there was any way at all that he could help with the case that he would be more than willing to give us a hand."

"If he was sincere, I think it would be wise on our part to ask if he would help. Although he can be grating on everyone's nerves, Moses is an excellent detective. As George said, this is not a simple case. We can use all of the experienced help we can get," Shipley said.

"Patrick Fucking Moses," Loftus said.

"Now, George, you know Moses had little to do with you being falsely held for the Prostitute Murders. You can thank Captain Morgan for that," Shipley said.

"I think he could have done a little more to get me out of that cage than he did," Loftus said.

"We can play this little game all day long if we want or we can do something about solving this case, before some other poor woman ends up dead."

"Sorry, Lieutenant. You're right," Loftus said.

"Harold, I need to you to get to New York to talk with Moses to get him back here as soon as you can. I don't want him to hem and haw over a cable," Shipley said.

"As soon as the coroner and I are done with our initial findings with Mrs. Casson I will be on my way to New York," Pinter said.

Shipley nodded again. "In that case, let's get the body and us out of this apartment before we need to be treated for something."

*****

New York

I was working late that night, doing I'm not sure what. Myrtle Robinson was long gone and I was alone in my back office; the front lights were out. I heard the front door open and close without much noise being made. There was no sound of footsteps. I reached into the top drawer of my desk and took out the revolver. I pointed it at the doorway.

"If you are here to kill me let's get it over with," I said. I didn't think Hanson would make an office visit, but I wasn't taking any chances.

The figure that stepped out of the shadows was recognizable even though the light wasn't good. The man was tall, wide shouldered and had a completely bald head. I didn't need light to tell me he was black.

"Custis?" I said.

The man stepped into the light of my office and it was indeed Flynn Colton's valet. His blank face, a look of indifference, scared me more than anything.

"I am not here to kill you," he said.

"That's comforting, "I said. I placed the gun on top of my desk, not far out of reach. "What do you want? Aren't you supposed to be guarding Flynn Colton?"

He didn't answer me and took a seat in one of my guest chairs. He rubbed one large hand across the top of his bald head. "Mr. Colton is at an appointment right now," he said. "I'm to pick him up at nine-thirty."

"A business appointment?" I probed.

"To his wife, yes. For Mr. Colton, no."

"A paramour?"

He sighed. "There are a lot of different names for a woman that would take up with a married man. Paramour might be one of the kindest."

I nodded. "So why are you here?"

"Mary Cobb told me that you wanted to speak with me."

The little maid had delivered on her promise to get Custis to talk with me. "I am trying to find the kidnapped Colton' children. I'm trying to find anyone who has an idea of who took them or where they might be."

He closed his eyes for a moment, concentrating or maybe praying. "When the War Between the States ended, I was ten years old. I had been on a plantation in Virginia; my parents were gone. I snuck onto a boat of Mr. Colton's father. He found me and when he discovered I was just some orphan slave he took me in. I stayed with Flynn's father whenever I could and worked on his ships. When Flynn was born in eighteen-seventy-six, he became my charge. I was responsible for his every move and his wellbeing. I have been with him ever since."

I shifted in my chair. Custis had his eyes closed again.

"I'd like to say that Flynn Colton is a good man, but that would be a lie. He started out as a good person, but business, and his father, corrupted him. Money corrupted him and women corrupted him. He is not fair in business. He is not a good man."

I took a deep breath. "Are you saying that you think someone that Flynn Colton does business with is responsible for taking the children?"

He shook his head. "No, sir. I don't believe so and I will only tell you so much."

"I'm sorry I interrupted."

"Mr. Colton no longer loves his wife. He has told me many times that she is no longer able to give him what he needs."

"Do you know what that might be?"

"Maybe. She is no longer twenty years old and her body has had the abuse of birthing three children. She also suffers from a malady that keeps her down a good amount of time. Her mood can be dark. She is constantly tired.

"In the past few years I have seen Mr. Colton stray farther from his home. He stays out late and it's hardly ever business related. He has recently met a young woman, a singer. He wants to be with her permanently."

"Why doesn't he just divorce Mrs. Colton? Money can't be that big of an object."

Custis laughed. "His father will not allow him to divorce. Too much of a stain on the family reputation."

"So he'll just go on seeing this singer on the side?"

"That would probably be the case unless Mrs. Colton needed to be institutionalized."

"So his antics are designed to push Mrs. Colton over the edge?"

I saw him nodding lightly and then it occurred to me. "You're telling me that Flynn Colton staged this kidnapping to drive Rebecca crazy?"

He got up suddenly from the chair he was sitting in. "I have probably told you too much already."

"Wait one minute. You can't leave."

"I have to go, sir. I have said too much and I must leave."

I stood and came around my desk quickly. Custis made a move as if to defend himself. "Do you know where these children are now?"

"I do not," he said. "I came here to tell you all of this because I believe the solution to all of this is right under your nose. You are a smart man, I hear. It's all right there. Press harder and you'll figure it out."

"Colton, when will he be at his house?"

"In the morning, before seven."

He turned to walk out of my office. I found myself shaking and I wasn't sure why. "Why did you decide to tell me this?"

He turned towards me. "I was raised to be a good person. I haven't seen much good in a while. I doubt I'll be with the Coltons much longer. My soul can't take it. It's best that I move along."

He left my office and I decided the best thing to do was reach Will Mannus first thing in the morning so we could catch Flynn Colton at his house and press him for information on the kidnapping. Custis had not told me everything and that bothered me, but he had told me enough to point me in the right direction.

*****

August 5th

I did not sleep well. What Custis had told me was rattling around in my head. The implications were clear; the reason not. I rolled over and stared hard at the clock on the dresser of my rented room in The Abbey hotel; I still hadn't found my own place. It read six-fifteen. I closed my eyes, hoping for a little more sleep before I had to get up to call Mannus. As soon as I closed them, the knocking started at my door. Then someone was calling my name.

I dragged myself out of bed, grabbing my gun along the way and quickly opened the door. There was a young patrolmen there, not more than twenty-five. He had a baby face and no whiskers. "What is it?" I said.

He blushed and swallowed hard. "Detective Mannus sent me to get you, sir," he said. "You're to come right away."

Suddenly I had a stabbing sensation at my temples, I blinked a few times and saw stars. My temples tightened. Thoughts of the Christmas morning when I had been summoned to Bubbly Creek to view the body of Eleanor Winter crossed my mind.

"Sir, are you alright?" the young cop asked.

"Yes. Of course. What is all the rush about?"

"It's the Colton children. They have been found in Battery Park."

It was the way he said it. "Alive, I hope?"

He lowered his eyes to the floor. "No, sir."

•   •   •

A man had been walking his two dogs along a path in Battery Park when a strong, foul scent hit him. The dogs both took off for a large stand of bushes. They both went into the bushes, howling, but came out and seemed down, as if something was wrong. As the man caught up with them the smell became stronger. Both dogs barked at a hole in the bushes, but they would not go in it. The man decided to investigate and soon came out of the bushes, vomiting up his breakfast.

Will Mannus, a couple of plainclothes cops and several in uniform were now standing near the bushes. Most seemed to be smoking cigarettes. None of the group were smiling.

"It's not a very pretty site," Mannus said.

I nodded. "I've seen some bad things," I said. For some reason I thought this gave me credence to view what was coming.

Mannus turned and entered the opening in the bushes. I followed and it was a little path that led to a circular opening in the small grove. In the middle of this opening were three small bodies. They were fully clothed in summer wear, but you could tell some animals had been at them. They'd also been there a while since the bodies, aided by the raging heat, had decomposed a good deal. They were all very dead and the cause of their death was no secret. Each child has been smashed on the head with a heavy object; their skulls had been crushed. Mannus pointed to his left. On the ground was a rock, about eight inches round. Even in the muted light I could see that it contained a good amount of blood on it.

"Seen enough?" Mannus asked quietly.

"More than."

He started back out of the grove. I was about to follow when the little bit of sun that we had reflected off something in the dirt. I knelt and saw a button, pearl colored, resting by the hand of the oldest girl, Maria. I picked it up and could see the imprint of a boat anchor on it. I swore to myself and put the button in my top pocket. I followed Mannus out of the opening.

It was only just past seven when we came out of those bushes and both of us were covered in drops of sweat. The heat was stifling again.

"I'm afraid this case will not have as good an outcome as the Hobbs' kidnapping," Mannus said. "Not only that, but we still have very little to go on."

I wiped my brow. "We have a lot more to go on than you would think," I said. "But we need to hurry."

"Moses, I like you, but what in the hell are you talking about?"

"If we can get one of your police vans we must hurry. I can tell you everything along the way. We also need someone to call the Colton residence to tell them we have news of the kidnapping and for no one to leave the house until we get there."

Mannus barked these instructions to one of the plainclothes detectives and soon the two of us were barreling along Seventh Avenue on our way to the Upper East Side. We got there a little before eight. I recounted to Mannus everything that had been told to me the night before by Custis. I showed him the button. By the time we got to the Colton residence, I could see that his temper was on full boil.

The Coltons were waiting for us in the sitting room on the first level. Flynn and Rebecca were sitting on a couch. Flynn was dressed in business attire; Rebecca wore a robe and looked worse than the day before. Her eyes were a raw red. Her hair look mangled. In her hand was the ever present handkerchief, soaked with tears.

The maid, Mary Cobb, was behind the couch. She looked nervous. Custis was in his usual place, taking up one of the corners of the room. His look never changed. There was no reading his feelings.

Flynn Colton stood when we walked into the room, led my Will Mannus. The look on Colton's face was shock, well played. "Tell us what you have found!" he demanded.

Mannus stopped and took a deep breath. "We have found the children's bodies."

There was a stillness in the room, deathly quiet. Rebecca Colton stood slowly. "Their bodies?"

"In Battery Park. I'm afraid they are dead," Mannus said.

Rebecca's face went blank and then she fainted, hitting the floor hard. Flynn rushed to his wife as did Mary Cobb. Custis left the room. As Mary tried to take care of Rebecca, Flynn rose. "Have you a suspect, yet?"

"We do," Mannus said.

"Have they been arrested?"

"May we see your suit closet, Mr. Colton?" I asked.

He looked at me, stunned. "My suit closet? Why on earth do you need to see my suit closet?"

"It may help us convict the killer," Mannus said.

Custis returned to the room with a pitcher of water and a glass. He knelt by Rebecca as Mary helped to revive her. "We'll need to get a doctor," Mary said.

"Custis, please make that call," Flynn Colton said. "I need to take the detectives upstairs for a moment."

Custis gave me a quick glance. "Yes, sir," he said, rising and leaving the room.

"Please follow me," Colton said. He led us out of the room and up the stairs to a huge bedroom with a large bed centered in it. In the rear of this room was a massive closet which held close to thirty or forty men's suits. "Here they are," he said.

I stepped past him and took the button I had found in Battery Park out of my pocket. I slowly checked each suit. Many were from Sailor and Sons. I had looked at fifteen or so when I found a brown pinstripe. The buttons on the front of the suit matched the one in my hand. They were all present. The first sleeve I lifted did not have a missing button. My stomach tightened a bit. I slowly lifted the second sleeve. The size of the buttons here were identical to the one I held. In the line of what was supposed to be four in a row was a missing button. I took the suit jacket off the hanger and showed Will Mannus. He nodded and turned to face Colton.

"Mr. Colton, you are the suspect we have been looking for and you are now under arrest for the murders of your three children."

· · ·

Flynn Colton was being held in a cell in the precinct building. His wife, Rebecca, was in the hospital and under the care of a physician. Mary Cobb, the maid, made the trip to the hospital with her. Custis was waiting for us in a small meeting room on the second floor. I wanted Mannus and me to talk to him before we talked to Colton. He was seated at the long, wooden table, looking dejected, and eyes staring straight ahead.

"You want something to drink, Custis?" I asked. "Maybe a glass of water?"

He shook his head slowly. "I'm fine."

Mannus took a seat to the side of him and lit a cigarette. He offered one to Custis, but got the slow head shake again. I remained standing.

"I have to tell you, Mr. …."

"Custis," the big man said. "I have always been just Custis."

Mannus turned his head to the side. "Wasn't that General Lee's wife's maiden name?"

"I believe so, sir."

"I have to tell you Custis that the way you answer these questions will have a tremendous bearing on the way that you are treated."

"I understand."

Mannus turned to me. "Patrick."

I cleared my throat. "You knew a lot more than you told me last evening."

"Not terribly much. I knew that Mr. Colton was behind the kidnappings. I knew his intent was to drive Mrs. Colton mad. I did not know that he intended to kill his children, his own children. What kind of person does that? Who can do that?" The look of strain on his face was palpable.

"Why don't you tell us what happened?" I said.

He took several deep breaths. With his imposing size, it was hard to believe how small he looked in that room. "Last Tuesday, in the mid-afternoon, Mr. Colton instructed me to take the carriage by Mrs. Marsh's house where she was watching the children. This was around three o'clock. The three children were playing out in the small yard. Mrs. Marsh was not present. Mr. Colton approached the gate and told his kids to come with him, that it would be alright, that he had a surprise for them. He told them he had cleared it with Mrs. Marsh. Well, this was their father, why wouldn't they come along? They all piled into the carriage and Mr. Colton told me to get to Battery Park, the south end, as soon as I could.

"We got to the park quickly. The children were well behaved, at least what I could hear. When I got to the park they all got out and Mr. Colton told me that he would be back in ten to fifteen minutes. He took them over a small rise in the landscape and towards a heavily wooded area. It was the last time I saw the children."

"He didn't tell you anything that he had planned?" I asked.

"Not a thing. They just started walking towards the trees and after a bit they were out of sight. I did as I was told and waited for Mr. Colton and the children to return to the carriage."

"How long did it take before he did return to the carriage?"

"At least a half an hour."

"And the children were not with him?"

Custis let out a short sob like sound. "No, sir. I asked him where they were and he told me he had left them with a friend. He told me he was very worried about Mrs. Colton's wellbeing and concerned with the children around her. The children needed to be away from her for a while. Of course, he told me that I was not to speak a word of this to anyone."

"How did he look?" Mannus asked.

"Looking back, I can say that he didn't look upset or anything. He looked calm. I've seen him come away from business meetings where he was upset. When he returned to the carriage, he didn't look like he had a care in the world."

"So he gets back to the carriage. What happens from there?" I asked.

"He told me to take him back to his office on the docks. That was where we went and we were there until about five o'clock when the call came that someone had taken the children from Mrs. Marsh's house."

"How did he act at that time?"

"I was told by one of his secretaries to have the carriage ready very soon to take Mr. Colton uptown. I was told that something had happened to his children. When he came into the garage area he looked shaken, very upset. He said we had to return home very quickly. He told me that his children had been kidnapped."

"And that was how the whole charade began?" Mannus said.

"Yes, sir. He acted surprised, shocked that something had happened to his children. In those first hours I even saw him cry a little. It was unbelievable."

I nodded. Custis was drained, sitting in that chair, wringing his hands together. "You had no idea what he was going to do to those children in that stand of woods?"

"None, sir. I am as loyal as they come, especially to the Colton family, but if I had any idea what was going to happen to those kids, it would not have happened."

"Why didn't you come forward to the police and tell them what you knew?"

He stared up at me for the longest moment. "I was sworn to secrecy for one thing. Secondly, I thought he had taken them to Battery Park and turned them over to someone, waiting until Mrs. Colton finally broke. Never in my mind did it occur to me that he had harmed those children in any way. It never once occurred to me…"

He stopped and burst into tears, dropping his head onto his arms on the table. His body shook violently as his emotions flooded out of him. I looked at Mannus and he nodded. We were done here. The only thing that Custis was guilty of was not telling anyone about the carriage ride to Battery Park and keeping it quiet for so long. It wouldn't have mattered anyway. By the time he would have told anyone what he knew, even a half hour after he'd witnessed it, those children had been murdered. We left an officer to keep watch over Custis. When he settled down and could compose himself the officer was to tell him that he was released.

• • •

The look that Flynn Colton wore said he was dazed. I wondered what he was dazed about. Was it that he did this all for a woman, that he had been caught or that he had murdered his children? I intended to find out.

He was sitting on a chair in the center of the cell. His hands were cuffed in front of him. He stared at us vacantly as we entered the cell. He seemed to be breathing normally. His body seemed to lack any tension at all.

"Will I be able to see Lenore soon?" he asked.

"Who the hell is Lenore?" Mannus snapped.

"It's a woman I have been seeing for some time. We have fallen in love. She is a singer."

"Oh, Jesus," Mannus said.

"I promised to meet her tonight," he said, eyes wandering from Mannus to me.

"All of your dates have been cancelled for some time," Mannus said.

"Why don't you tell us what happened?" I asked. "We know that you intended to stage a kidnapping to push Rebecca to madness. What happened to derail those plans?"

"They weren't there. I paid them a thousand dollar deposit and they didn't show up. I guess I panicked when they didn't show up." His eyes shot up to me, bulging. "I wasn't going to kill them, but when they didn't show up I didn't know what to do. I promised Lenore I would divorce Rebecca. I needed the kids gone to get her to crack. She would have. Then I could have divorced her. They were supposed to watch the children, care for them, until it was over. They never showed up and then the kids started to complain. I took them into that clearing in the bushes. Little Flynn started to cry and I was so mad that I picked up this rock and hit him on the head. Then I hit Constance. Maria, she started to yell at me and grabbed at me. She was trying to stop me. That must have been when she tore the button off my suit coat. I was finally able to hit her. I checked them all. They were all dead. I left them in that bunch of bushes and returned to the carriage."

Mannus' mouth was hanging open at the admission. Not that Colton admitted it, but the casualness of the discussion. It was like he was describing a shipping transaction. Mannus and I had talked of evil, but this wasn't evil. This was madness.

"When my father returns from Europe he will straighten this all out. Whatever it costs he will take care of it. It's important, you see. I need to see Lenore."

Will Mannus took one step forward and slapped Flynn Colton with the back of his hand. Colton and the chair toppled to the side. "The next fucking person you see will be the hangman," Mannus said.

"Please let me see Lenore," Flynn Colton said.

. . .

Lenore Anthony performed nightly at the Mid-town Club, not far from the Broadway theatre district. Mannus and I watched her show from some very close seats. She was a beautiful woman, tall, big chested and flowing blonde hair. I could definitely see what Colton saw in her. When her first act was over we went backstage to talk to her during the intermission.

"Of course I know Flynn Colton," she said. "He's a big fan. Comes to my show just about every night. See those," she said, pointing to a vase with blooming, long stemmed roses. "He sends flowers all the time. And candy."

"Sounds like a pretty big fan," Mannus said.

It must have been the way he said it because she looked at him kind of funny. "What are you getting at, detective?"

"Are you sure it was no more that Colton being a big fan?"

She smiled at Mannus and reached behind her. In a small frame that sat on her table was a photograph of a little boy, maybe two. He was a cute little guy. "This is who I am in love with, my son Johnny. His father watches him so I can sing here at night and save money to get a house outside of the city. We're getting close, but it will still take some time."

"And Flynn Colton," I asked, "what were his plans?"

"He showed up one night, front row, and started coming pretty much every night. He'd send the flowers, the candy and other gifts. He asked me to dinner and drinks, but I told him I was married. I told him I was happily married. I must have told him no fifty times, but he kept asking. He was always polite, never pushy or rude. I just kept saying no. If he had bothered me I would have reacted differently, but he always left me alone."

"Never more than a fan?" Mannus asked.

"That was it," she said. "Maybe one with a big crush, but that was it."

"You never talked about him getting a divorce from his wife? About maybe getting together after he was divorced?" I said.

She burst out laughing and had to dab at tears that were coming from her eyes. "I get asked out a lot, by a lot of different men. Some have a lot of money like Flynn Colton, but I could care less. I have my husband and my little boy. That's plenty for me. A couple of more years of this club and then I will be gone."

. . .

So what did Flynn Colton's fabricated story of love do to us? We returned to our table and we watched the second half of the show. Lenore wasn't a great singer; she wasn't bad. What she had was alluring beauty. This was what had transfixed Colton. This was what devised the plan in his mind that by getting rid of the children his wife would go crazy. Unfortunately, it all went wrong when the people who were supposed to care for the children didn't show up at Battery Park.

"Do you think there were really people who were supposed to come along and take the children from him?" Mannus asked.

I shook my head. "I'm guessing we'll never find out."

The other thing that happened was that my good friend, the pressure at my temples, and the aura of light came back. My head felt like someone was applying a vise on the sides. I closed my eyes for a moment as Lenore sang and it felt better.

"Whiskey?" Mannus asked. "We're off duty."

I hadn't had a drop in nearly eight months. I was convinced that the evil deeds of the Levee led me to alcohol and opium. Here it was madness. Madness made Colton envision that future with Lenore. Madness made him kill his children. All for, it seemed, not a fucking thing.

I smiled. "Whiskey."

So we drank. It was easy how after the burn of the first glass the amber liquid slid so silkily down my throat. My temples loosened and the light aura went away. Lenore sounded better and looked fantastic. Her show ended and a vaudeville act took over. There were some funny bits, some that were racy and a couple of raunchy ones. We laughed and drank through most of it.

"I forgot to tell you," Mannus leaned over and said into my ear. I could smell his cigarettes and whiskey breath. "Your boy Hanson has been spotted at a place called Dagger's Inn down in Five Points."

A flare of something hot roared up my neck and into the base of my skull. "Why the fuck are we sitting here?"

"I could use a diversion," Mannus said. "Finish your whiskey."

I drank up and grabbed Mannus by the arm as we got up to leave. We both staggered a bit. "This guy has a habit of killing my partners."

He smiled. "Then maybe we should kill him."

• • •

Dagger's Inn was a small pub on the south end of Five Points. To say that everyone in the place was a hard case would be an understatement. They all knew we were cops the moment we walked into the place and they cut us a wide birth. No one seemed to want any trouble this night. The bartender was a small, wiry guy with a nasty scar on the left side of his cheek. He had thinning, gray hair that he wore combed back. A cigarette dangled from his lips as he washed glasses behind the bar.

Mannus placed his badge on the bar and the man looked at it, but kept on cleaning the dishes. "Two whiskeys," Mannus said.

The barkeep poured the whiskey into two glasses. He still hadn't looked at us. He pushed the drinks towards us. "On the house," he said.

"We're looking for a guy named Christian Hanson," Mannus said. "We've heard from good sources that he's been in here quite a bit lately."

Again, the glass washing. "Don't know anyone by that name."

"He's a big, broad shouldered, son of a bitch," I said. "Tall, blonde hair, parted down the middle. Doesn't talk."

The bartender lifted his eyes to me. "Doesn't talk?"

"He's a mute," I said.

"Doesn't sound familiar."

With that I quickly reached across the bar and grabbed the bastard by his tie and collar and dragged him across the bar for a good look at me. With my other hand I stuck the barrel of my gun in his ear hole.

There was a mad scrambling of people and chairs all around us as people did their best to get out of the way. Mannus drew his gun and did a quick look around the place. So far no one was stepping in to help out.

"Are you sure it doesn't sound familiar?" I asked the frightened bartender.

"He's been here a few times, but I hear he left town," he said quickly. "Someone said the heat from that shooting was getting turned up. I haven't seen him in days."

I pulled the gun out of his ear. He wasn't lying. "Left town?" a weak version of my voice asked.

"That's what I heard. Went back to Chicago."

"Chicago," I said outloud, but to myself.

I eased him back over the bar and holstered my gun. I didn't say anything to Mannus, but he knew how I felt. I walked out of the bar to the waiting police van with Mannus following. This whole night, for lack of a better way to describe it, had turned to shit.

• • •

In my office, on the top of a cabinet for files, was a bottle of good Canadian whiskey and one glass. I left it there as a reminder of how bad things had been. I didn't care that night about the past, or really, the future. I only cared about now. Right now, things were not going as planned. I opened the bottle and poured a fair amount into the glass. It went down much too easily. I repeated this procedure at least three times that I remember. After that, it was kind of a blank.

*****

August 6th

I heard my name being said. I heard it said more than once. Whoever was saying it sounded a little distressed. Then there was some pulling and pushing on my body. Everything seemed amplified from the sound to the poking and prodding I was receiving. My head hurt. I moved it a little and was struck with a lightning bolt of pain directly between the eyes. I tried to open them. It was light in my office but my sight only registered shadows. There was more name calling and more prodding. I quickly sat up in my chair and tried to open my eyes. This was my first mistake of the day.

I felt dizzy and grabbed the little garbage can near my desk and threw up all of that good whiskey or at least what was left of it. This little action caused my head to revolt with thunderous throbs and deep knifelike stabs to my neck. I was sure that I was near death. After I emptied my stomach, my ribs ached. I sat back up.

"Mr. Moses, are you okay?"

I stared ahead and my eyes focused. Myrtle Robinson was there and she looked aghast. I tried to talk, but my mouth didn't appear to be working correctly. There was also a grimy, dirty taste in there.

"Water," I managed to say weakly.

"I'll get you some water," Myrtle said and she left my field of vision. I wanted to put my head back down, but I knew if I did it might not come up again. On my desk was an empty whiskey bottle and one glass, my partners in crime.

Myrtle returned with a clean glass of water. She handed it to me and I took a couple of sips. The cold water felt like life was being injected back into my lifeless body. "Mr. Moses, what could have happened to make you slide so quickly?" Myrtle asked.

The thought of explaining the whole Flynn and Lenore tale made my head throb again. When I thought of Hanson running away to Chicago I had to reach for the garbage can again, but this time I only gagged.

"You have a visitor."

I looked up at her and I could tell from the way she looked at me that she was both hurt and feeling sorry for me, maybe like a mother. "We are closed today," I said.

"He claims he is a friend."

"Then he'll understand it when you tell him that I can't see him."

"He's from Chicago."

I finished the water from the glass and handed it to her. The thought occurred to me that I wasn't going to die, but this did little to make me feel any better. "More water and send him in," I said.

Her eyes narrowed. "More water and send him in what?"

I took a deep breath, but that wasn't a great idea. All I could smell was booze and sweat, all emanating from me. "More water and send him in please."

She smiled. "That's more like it."

She left the office and I hung my head a bit and closed my eyes. Why did I drink? To get drunk. I had accomplished that goal. I wondered how long I would have to struggle. I righted my head and opened my eyes. Standing in front of me was a diminutive fellow with balding hair and thick eyeglasses. His suit was rumpled and my guess was that this had occurred during his travels.

"Good morning, Patrick," he said. "You heard I was coming and you celebrated?"

"Harold, you picked a fine day to come and visit me."

"My train was in late last night. I got here as soon as I could," Harold Pinter said.

"Did someone give you the impression that I needed help?"

"I only got that impression after I saw you. It is actually the other way around. It is I that needs help from you."

Myrtle came back in the office and placed the new glass of water in front of me. "Mr. Pinter," she said. "Would you like something to drink?"

"I am fine, Mrs. Robinson. I had a very nice breakfast before I came over here."

My eyes were better now and it didn't hurt to have them open or to move my head around. Pinter looked the same to me, but the mystery persisted. Why was he here?

"Harold, what did you come all the way to my office in New York to ask me?" I grabbed the water and slurped down half the glass.

Harold looked over at Myrtle and then at me.

"She can stay," I said. "She's kind of like my partner."

"Underpaid and under loved partner," she said.

"Partners are never happy," I said.

Harold ran a hand through his thinning hair and pushed his glasses up on the bridge of his nose. "I sent you a telegram not too long ago about a case that we had. It was the murder of an older woman, probably close to eighty. She had been tied up in her little apartment using her own bed sheets which had been cut into strips. Other remnants of the sheet had been used to blindfold her and to gag her mouth. Pieces of her pillow had been stuffed into her mouth. She either suffocated or had a heart attack."

My head hurt and I was still dehydrated. I drank more water. "I seem to remember something about that."

"Well, I hoped you would. You indicated you would help if you could."

I closed my eyes and held them shut for a moment. "First, you wrote me about this case, and now you come all the way to New York to ask me for assistance."

"It's not one case," Harold Pinter said. "It's now two cases. The other occurred the day before yesterday. We now have two cases, same modus operandi. One just outside the Levee; the other near Lincoln Park."

"Two dead older women?"

"About the same age and killed in an identical fashion."

I finished the water and my head didn't seem to hurt as much as I concentrated on what Harold had said. "What kind of help do you want from me?"

Harold cleared his throat. "We would like you to come back to the

Levee and assist us with this case. We fear we may have a bit of an epidemic on our hands."

"A repeat killer?"

"If that is the correct term."

"Whose idea was this?"

"Lieutenant Shipley. He ran it by the others and they concur."

"Shipley?"

"He's the interim in charge of the precinct. There's been a tremendous caseload on the detectives and they are stretched very thin. It would be a big service to us if you came back."

"Reinstated?"

"Full Detective rank and pay."

"The pay will never sway me. Let me think it over," I said.

"I need to return with you," Harold said bluntly.

Before I could respond, Myrtle Robinson spoke up. "That sounds like an awful case, Mr. Moses, one that your friends could use a little help with. Go for a while and see what you can do. I will hold things down here. When you are done in Chicago you can come back here."

I looked at Harold who was smiling widely. "My partner thinks I should help you out so I guess I will. When do we go?"

"There's a train at four o'clock today."

I considered my current physical shape. I had about six hours to get ready for the journey. "Let's find out who's killing these women."

• • • •

If there is a term to describe the long train ride to Chicago it would be lost time. For most of the ride through the dark I slept. My condition didn't warrant much more activity. When I was awake, I managed to only eat two dry pieces of toast and drink a lot of water. Harold Pinter gave me some tablets that he swore would ease the pain at my temples. All they did was upset my stomach, leading me to belch for an hour, and make me thirstier. I was happier when I was asleep.

When I was awake for the ride, Pinter recanted the tale to me of the two women who had been murdered with their own bedsheets, one down near the Levee, another in Lincoln Park. Harold said they had little clues and maybe the other detectives handling the case could tell me more once we got to Chicago. That explanation was fine with me. My damaged brain and body couldn't take a lot more.

When we got to Chicago, Harold dropped me and my bags off in a rented apartment on Twenty-Fourth Street. It would do until I could find another place, if I stayed long enough. I put my things away and crawled into the creaky bed. I slept soundly until the next morning.

*****

August 7th

When I stood outside of the Twenty-Second Precinct the next morning, I had mixed feelings about what I was getting myself into. I stood near the statue of Grant where a prostitute had once had her head impaled. That thought alone made a shiver run up my back. I had been fine in New York, building a business based on the domestic crimes of life and then along came a kidnapping that turned into a brutal murder. Did this make it okay for me to return to the Levee and its special breed of insanity? This is where Simon Kluge and Thomas Morgan tried to rid the world of prostitutes, one by one. This is the home of corrupt aldermen who rule the land like kings. It's a place where drugs, alcohol and whores are a way of life. It was also the place where someone was snuffing out old women and where my nemesis Christian Hanson had probably returned.

"Are you just going to stand there and look at the fucking building or are you going to go in?" a voice behind me said.

I turned and there stood George Loftus. The last time I had seen him was while he was waiting for indictment in the bowels of the building after being falsely accused as being the Prostitute Murderer. I knew he would be vindicated when I shot Thomas Morgan to death. "Hello, Loftus."

George lit a cigarette and took a giant puff. He was eyeing me warily. "You know, I could have died in that damn cell. You could have done a lot more to get me out of there sooner."

I thought on this for a moment. "You wouldn't have died, and, anyway, I had to make sure that I had the right person."

He sniffed at the warm, morning air. "Well, the building, the people in it, and the Levee haven't changed that much since you've been gone. Since you've decided to grace us with your presence you might as well get inside and see what you can do about the old ladies."

I winced a bit. "Is that the best you can do to describe them?"

He shrugged. "For now, that's about it. Two old women, living alone and seemingly no one to turn to. A fucking sad existence and a terrible way to go."

I looked up at the two story building again. "You're right. Not that much is going to get done standing here. Might as well step inside."

"One more thing, Moses."

"What's that?"

Loftus extended a hand to me. "Welcome back."

• • •

I was a bit surprised by the warm welcome that I received inside the building. Most of the beat cops were the same and many shook my hand and patted me on the back. Riley O'Donnell came by and said hello. He wanted to make sure that Loftus and I had made up. When I told him we had he seemed relieved. Harold came out of his lab in the basement and, even though he had seen me, looked happy that I had actually shown up at the precinct. One of the last people to shake my hand was a young man, mid-twenties, tall with a receding hairline of brown hair. He looked nervous and didn't do a good job of looking me in the eyes when we shook.

"Your name again?" I asked.

"Keenan Coughlin," he said quietly.

"Like the alderman?" I asked.

"He is my uncle."

Why, I don't' know, was there suddenly that pushing against my temples. Before I could respond to young Keenan, he had made his way to the back of the group. My head eased and I was told there would be a meeting in Lieutenant Shipley's office in ten minutes. Why that didn't cause tension, I don't know. Perhaps I was adapting.

"Welcome back, Moses."

This was the greeting I received from Lieutenant Shipley. He was standing behind his desk as the small group filed into his office for the briefing on the two murdered older women. It had only been eight months, but Shipley hadn't changed. He stood erect, in full uniform, with his shirt pinching him at the neck. More than anything I remembered the high-pitched voice. That hadn't gone anywhere.

"You're all aware that Detective Moses has offered to come back and help us with these investigations," Shipley continued. "While here, he will be reinstated to his rank of detective. I think it's important for Detective Moses to know everything we've got so that he can get involved right away. Detective O'Donnell."

I had never heard Riley called anything but Riley and he looked uncomfortable as he stood to address the small group. I noticed there was food on his already dirty tie. "The first victim was Grace Muldor," Riley said quietly. "Her apartment was at Wabash and Twenty-Sixth. She was eighty-three years old and as far as we can tell there are no living relatives. It's no secret that she was tied to a chair in her living room with her own bedsheets. Bits of sheet were than used to blindfold her and gag her mouth. Under the mouth gag, a bit of a pillow was stuffed into her mouth. According to Harold and the coroner, death was caused by suffocation. The last person to see her alive was her caretaker who comes in five days a week. She was there the day before. Ms. Muldor had been fine and in good spirits."

"What about the neighbors in her building?" I asked. "No one heard or saw anything?"

"No, Patrick. We asked everyone in her building and everyone in several nearby buildings. Nothing."

"The killer used a small pair of shears that were in the kitchen to cut up the bedsheet," Harold said. "They also helped themselves to a cake that was also in the kitchen."

"They?" I asked. "As in two?"

"There were two dirty forks near the cake pan. We can only assume."

"That's it?"

"For that case," Shipley said. "Detective Loftus will give us the briefing on Dorothy Casson."

Loftus stood slowly. "Mrs. Casson was eighty-one years old and lived by herself in a first floor flat in Lincoln Park. The cops in the local precinct caught the case and called us in when they heard there were similarities. The body had been sitting a bit by the time we got there, but it's the same story. Cut up bedsheets were used to bind her to a chair, blindfold her and gag her mouth. Again a pillow was torn up to stuff in her mouth. All of the neighbors were asked and nobody saw anything. Unlike Mrs. Muldor, no cake was eaten. In both cases, I think it's important to note, it doesn't appear that anything was taken. Neither apartment was tossed. Everything looked rather tidy."

"So the motive is?" I asked.

There was silence and then someone cleared their throat. I turned and saw Keenan Coughlin looking at me, blushing.

"Yes, Coughlin."

"The motive, at least it seems to me, is murder for pleasure," he said.

I thought for a moment as the whole room stared at me. "At least for the time being. Robbery and theft are out. Maybe these women were killed for some sort of revenge, but we have nothing that tells us that the women knew each other."

"Nothing," Loftus said.

"Then I think that is out as well. I think what we have is a killer or killers who are murdering these women because he likes it. Did Mrs. Casson have any relatives?"

George flipped through some notes. "A sister up in Milwaukee who is ninety-one. She thinks Lincoln is still the president."

"Harold?" I said.

"We have a killer, or killers as you say, that has killed two older women in a similar fashion. There appears to be no motive other than the killing itself. No witnesses saw or heard anything at either site. Someone ate some cake at Mrs. Muldor's but maybe it was her. That's about it."

"So we don't really have very much?" I said aloud.

There was no answer from anyone so I took that as an affirmation. We had two elderly women who were suffocated with their own bedsheets and pillows in their apartments. No one saw or heard anything. Our only clue was that the killer or killers liked cake. I didn't think that narrowed our suspects down very much. My temples tightened.

. . .

Shipley asked that I stay behind after the meeting broke up. I also noticed that young Keenan Coughlin had not left the small office. Shipley remained standing, his pinched neck looking redder as I got closer to him.

"This is quite a challenge for the precinct, Moses," he said rather quietly.

"I think it would be a challenge for anyone when you have two murdered women and not one clue telling you which direction to go in."

"That's true, but as you know the criminals don't always make it easy for us."

I knew Shipley hadn't been much of a street cop, but I smiled as I played along.

"For that reason," he said, "I have decided to give you a little help with the case, someone to do the necessary little things that you don't have time to do."

I let out a deep sigh. "Who might that be?" I asked, knowing all along.

"I would like Mr. Coughlin to help you. He scored exceptionally well at the academy for new recruits and has shown a great aptitude in all of his field assignments."

I didn't look at Coughlin. "Does young Mr. Coughlin know anything about the history of my past two partners?"

"I do, sir," Keenan said confidently. "They were both killed by a man named Christian Hanson."

"Before I left New York I received word that Hanson, who was being sought for a shooting out there, had left town and was headed back to Chicago. I think he is probably in this area as we speak."

Shipley raised his eyes at that. "That has nothing to do with the case we are working on."

"True, but he is still the prime suspect in the murder of two police officers, as well as others."

58

"You may leave, Keenan," Shipley said brusquely. "Please close the door behind you."

I heard the young detective's feet against the hard floor and then the closing of the door.

"Moses, there are a few things that I would like to be clear with you about."

"I am all ears, Lieutenant."

He smirked. "I want the majority of your time spent on trying to figure out who killed these two women. I can't tell you not to keep an eye out for Hanson, but your priority are these two murders."

"I understand," I said.

"Secondly, there is an aide to Chief Collins who seems to think that you may have had something to do with the murder of your father as well as that of Amos Stokes. The timing of these two murders comes close to the end of two investigations that you were involved in. It also appears that both men were shot at close range using a revolver similar to the ones we provide our officers and detectives with."

I swallowed hard.

"This aide's name is Captain Jack Garfield. He is a belligerent, harsh man. For some reason, I don't know why, he has you tabbed as a cold blooded killer. He was against bringing you back into the fold. This whole idea might not have worked if it hadn't been for Aldermen Coughlin."

"Coughlin?"

"As much as he seems to despise you he is also very impressed as some of the cases you have solved. When he heard you were might be coming back he asked Chief Collins if his nephew could possibly work with you. Collins agreed and Garfield's inquiry into your involvement in the two shootings has been slowed down a bit. Chief Collins knows we can use you on this case and at the same time help out the alderman."

I let out a breath. "I am glad to be of service."

Shipley gave me one of his better, thin-lipped smiles. "And we are glad to have you, but a word of caution."

"Yes, Lieutenant."

"Keep an eye out for Garfield. He is remarkably dogged in the matters he pursues. It may be his only enviable trait."

"But I thought his investigation had been tempered, even though there is nothing to investigate."

"Officially, but he can be an unrelenting aggressor."

I nodded.

"And Moses, one more thing. As difficult as it might be for you, please try and refrain from shooting anyone while you are back in the Levee. I have also pledged my somewhat good word to Chief Collins that I would keep you in control, and that includes opium and alcohol, so please keep that in mind."

"I will only shoot those where I have no other choice and who truly have it coming to them."

He stretched his pinched neck and smiled again. "You may go now, Moses."

•   •   •

I walked down the stairs of the building to the area where they had the holding cells. I had seen George Loftus held here and also where Frank Pelicanos, the man who said he murdered my father, had hanged himself. I wondered how Sylvia, his wife, and her two children were doing. I promised to look in on them.

Harold Pinter was busy looking at something intently on his desk. When he was working it was hard to get his attention. I knocked loudly on the door that was open. He looked up at me. "Oh, hello Patrick. Hello Keenan."

I hadn't noticed Keenan Coughlin follow me downstairs. I was about to remand him, but then remembered that he was now my partner.

"As far as murder weapons go, you said that torn bedsheets were used to bind the victims and eventually suffocate them," I said.

Harold moved to a small table to the left of his desk. He picked up a strip of cloth and held it out to me. It looked like it had come from a common, white bedsheet.

"I didn't say torn bedsheets," he said. "These strips are all pretty much the same. They are all about the width of the sheet and about three inches wide."

"What do you mean they weren't torn?"

"Look closely. They all appear to have been cut by scissors or shears and done very neatly. The cutting is in even, straight lines, the strips symmetrical."

"And what does that mean?"

"Our killer was meticulous in his work."

"And not in any fit of passion or rage," Keenan said.

Again, I was going to criticize my young associate, but Harold beat me to it. "What do you mean, Keenan?"

He cleared his throat. His face blushed. "To me, the killer was taking his time when making the sheet strips. He wasn't in any violent frame of mind, not in any hurry. I would say he was very calm, in no hurry."

Harold nodded. "Excellent observation."

"What does that tell us?" I asked.

Harold tilted his head a little to one side. "Our killer may lack much of a conscience."

• • •

Keenan and I grabbed a carriage in front of the precinct and I told the driver to go to Paris, a brothel on the northern edge of the Levee.

"Why are we going to a brothel?" Keenan asked.

"That is where Big Jim Colosimo has his office. I want to know if he has any idea where my old friend Christian Hanson might be."

"We're looking for Hanson already?

"I'm always looking for Hanson," I said quickly.

Keenan blushed. "Jim Colosimo knows him?"

"He did some freelance work for Colosimo last year. If Hanson came back here, he might look up Big Jim for work again."

I noticed for the first time how stagnant and moist the air was, rift with humidity. It was like riding through steam. My shirt was damp already and we'd only been outside a few minutes.

"Is there anything that you would like me to look into on the case?" Keenan asked.

That was a good question. Where do you look when your clues are bedsheet strips and chocolate cake? Where do you look when no one has seen or heard anything, yet two women are dead? There didn't seem to be anywhere to look. "I think, for the time being, that you should do as much legwork as you can to try and find Hanson?"

"Hanson? What has he got to do with this case?"

"Not a thing, but he will eventually cross paths with us. If it is on our terms it will be to our advantage. If it's on his terms we could be in trouble. He is a very dangerous man."

"I will ask around?"

"Leave no rock unturned. He is the lowest form of life."

Keenan nodded. "Anything else?"

"Yes. There is a cop at headquarters, a captain. His name is Jack Garfield. Apparently he does not have a warm spot in his heart for me and thinks I'm a murderer. Please ask around and see what you can find out about him, good or bad."

"Yes, sir," Keenan said.

"And knock off that shit. Call me Patrick."

Keenan smiled broadly.

"Your uncle really asked for me to help train you? I thought he hated me."

"Not at all. He doesn't think you two would ever be great friends, but he is an admirer of your work. He thinks you are a great detective."

"And I think that Alderman Coughlin has completely mastered the art of running the First Ward."

• • • •

Big Jim Colosimo was in his office when we arrived at Paris, but his secretary said it would be a few moments before he could see us. I told her it was important, but this had little effect on her. She smiled and went back to writing out correspondence for her boss. Keenan and I waited quietly.

After no more than ten minutes, the door to Big Jim's office opened and the large Italian stepped into his lobby. He was wearing an all -white suit with a red tie. On each finger of his hands there was a glittering, gold ring. His hair was professionally cut and styled. "I thought I would see you back here, Moses. I just didn't think it would be so damn soon."

We didn't shake hands, but he did lead us back into his inner office where we took seats in front of his massive desk. He asked if we wanted any drinks, but we both declined.

"So, Keenan," Jim asked, "your uncle has made sure you were placed with one of the department's finest."

"Yes, sir."

Big Jim laughed. "He is also a prick and a very large pain in the ass. By the way, Moses, Margaret Krause will no longer make dresses for my wife. She believes that her friendship with our family may have been part of the reason her husband was beaten to death."

I winced at those words. Gunter Krause, my former partner, beaten to death in an alley behind a Bed Bug Row whorehouse, hadn't been gone that long.

I could tell Jim could see what his words had done to me. "For some reason, I don't think you came to me to talk about Margaret or her husband."

"I heard that our old friend, Christian Hanson, may have returned to Chicago."

Colosimo sighed heavily. "Now we're back to Hanson again?"

"Apparently he shot a bartender down in the Five Points area of New York. The heat was getting to be too much so he left town. Word is he came back to Chicago."

Colosimo picked up a small file from his desk top and began to work at his finger nails. He reviewed his work and his eyes came back to me. "Moses, I know this man Hanson had a hand in killing two of your partners. I also know he is a violent and unpredictable character, a scary man. Since I know that you are now back in town and are going to be diligent in finding him, do you think I would be dumb enough to associate with him?"

"I don't think you're dumb at all, Jim. I only just arrived back in town. I think Hanson beat me back here by a couple of days. Seen or heard anything about him?"

Big Jim smiled. "Not a thing."

"Would it be too much to ask that you let us know if you do hear anything about him?"

"I don't really like you, Moses. I find you arrogant, but since I still feel badly about what happened to Margaret Krause and her family, and I'd like to help out a relative of Alderman Coughlin, I'll keep my eyes and ears open."

"That would be very nice of you," I said.

.   .   .

Later that day I found myself stupidly looking at the house that Frank and Sylvia Pelicanos had lived in. The temperature was pushing ninety and the sun was glaring like a fierce, orange ball. All of the grass and any little bushes in front of the house were mostly brown and looked like they'd flare up in flames if ignited. It didn't look like anyone was residing in the house.

I walked up the front stairs and couldn't believe how nervous I felt. I know Sylvia held me responsible for her husband's death even though he had hanged himself. Why the man claimed he killed my father was another story, a sick man's story.

I knocked on the door loudly and took several deep breaths to calm myself. After the third time I knocked the door was opened by a woman, not Sylvia. She was short and squat, dark haired and looked angry. "What is it?" she asked.

"I'm looking for Sylvia Pelicanos," I said sheepishly.

"Doesn't live here anymore," the woman said. Her eyes were rimmed with red.

"Do you know what happened to her?"

"What I know is I have to work the night shift and talking to you is cutting into my sleep." She started to close the door, but I stuck my foot in the way. Her look showed defiance, but that softened when I stuck my badge in her face.

"I'm just trying to find out what happened to her and then I'll be gone."

"Why didn't you tell me you were a cop?"

"This isn't police business."

"My family owns this house. The Pelicanos lady couldn't pay the rent after her husband died. She had to move out, and before you ask, I'll tell you I have no idea where she went. She told my brother that she hated Chicago, what it did to her husband and her family. My brother was pretty sure she was leaving town."

I wasn't surprised at what she said. I had sent Sylvia a significant amount of money, but I guess she decided this city was not the place to raise her family. I couldn't blame her. I thanked the woman and started for my new home.

• • • •

The building I was residing in was three stories and held six apartments. There were four concrete steps leading to a small porch. My apartment was bigger than I needed, on the second floor, with a nice view of the street and the large oak in front of the place. What got my attention more than anything was the boy who was sitting on the steps. He was about ten, red headed and with abundant freckles.

"You lost," I said.

"Nope," he said. "Me and my mom live here on the second floor."

"That's nice. I'm in the unit next to you."

"The landlord told my mom you were a cop."

I smiled. "That's true. I'm a detective."

He sized me up for a minute. "You ever shoot anybody?"

My recent record was loaded with shootings, some not very legal. "I try not to use my gun," I said defensively.

"My name is Freddie Winston," he said.

"Patrick," I answered.

"My mom is Lois. She works as a nurse over at Mercy. She told me to wait out here until she came home. She should be along in a bit. You want to come to dinner, Patrick? We're having a ham."

Whenever I think about hams I remember what Gunter had told me about the slaughter operation at the Yards and the way they handled pigs. I get a little nauseous. "You think you'd better ask your mom first before inviting a stranger to dinner?"

"My mom was the one who said that if you were a nice man that we should invite you for dinner."

"Well, in that case, how can I refuse?"

"I'll come over and knock on your door when dinner is ready. It shouldn't be too long."

"That sounds wonderful," I said. With that, I climbed the stairs to my apartment. I took off my suit jacket and shoes and sat in the most comfortable chair in the place. It wasn't long before I was feeling my eyes begin to drift off. The last few days had finally caught up to me.

I don't know how long I was out for, but I was in a deep sleep when I heard the knocking at my door. It took a moment for me to get my bearings, but finally I was out of the chair and answering the door. There stood little Freddie Winston with a worried look on his face.

"What's wrong?" I asked, stretching some of the stiffness out of my shoulders.

"I didn't think you were home," Freddie said. "I told my mom you were coming for dinner and then I thought you weren't here."

"Sorry, Freddie. I just dozed off in the chair for a bit. Is dinner ready now?"

"It is."

"Okay. Tell you what. Give me a few minutes to wash up and I'll be right over."

Ten minutes later, I only had to knock once on their door and it was opened quickly by Freddie. I was led into a small dining area just outside of the kitchen. There was a small table with three place settings at it. In the middle of the table was a vase with a number of fresh cut, yellow flowers in it. There were also two bowls. One held mashed potatoes; the other green beans. Lastly there were two glasses of red wine. I was still recovering from my whiskey binge in New York and wasn't looking forward to drinking for a while. That was until I saw Lois Winston.

I could see where Freddie got the red hair and the freckles. He was a male spitting image of his mother. Lois wasn't very tall, wore her hair short, and had on a light blue dress. In her hands she carried a platter with thick pieces of sliced ham. She smiled at me, nice white teeth.

"Mr. Moses, welcome to our home," she said.

I don't know why I didn't think she'd be pretty, but this was even wrong. She was very pretty. "Thank you for having me. When Freddie asked me, I wasn't sure what to think."

"Why not? You're our new neighbor. Isn't it neighborly to ask your neighbors over for dinner?"

I hadn't thought that about my former neighbors in the Levee. I thought most of them might rob me. "I guess it is."

"Why don't you sit at the head of the table and Freddie can take the spot on your right and I'll sit over here."

I did as I was told and soon Lois was serving food to the three of us. I thought there might be some sort of corny neighborly toast, but that didn't happen. As soon as the food was on their plates the Winstons were digging in. I followed suit. Maybe it was Lois Winston, but I forgot everything Gunter had told me about pigs and I ate everything on my plate. I also finished my wine and watched as Lois refilled my glass. For the most part, we ate in near silence. When we were done eating, Lois sent Freddie into another room to play. She smiled at me and I returned it.

"So what made you return to Chicago?" she said.

Maybe it was my training as a cop, but certain things you hear tend to tip you off to something. "How did you know I'd been gone?"

Again she smiled and poured a little more wine into my glass. "My mother once told me that it was rude to answer a question with another question."

"Sorry for being rude," I said. I took a sip of the wine. "I just didn't remember telling Freddie anything about my past."

"Oh, it wasn't Freddie."

Now I was really on guard. "Who might it have been?"

She smiled again and touched the top of my left hand. Her hand was very warm. "You probably don't remember me, but I was working the night your friend Luigi, the priest, was brought in with his heart attack. I felt so bad for you with the vigil you took as he struggled that night."

That night had been over eight months ago; Luigi, the first of many of my friends to die that winter. "I see, but I was around town for a while after Luigi died. How did you know I'd left town?"

"We also treated another person who you had contact with. Do you remember Beth Stokes?"

I nodded slowly. Beth Stokes had been a key witness in the case that proved that Frank Pelicanos had not shot my father. When word of her relationship with Pelicanos got out, her husband Amos beat her and sent her to Mercy. I paid Amos a visit shortly after that and shot him in the throat in his bedroom. I went to New York right after that.

Now, Captain Jack Garfield was looking at me for that murder.

"You're doing a lot of thinking," Lois said.

"I'm sorry. I've had a lot going on recently."

"You nodded when I mentioned Beth Stokes."

"She was a witness in a case of mine. Her involvement got her beat up by her husband."

She sipped her wine and ran her tongue across her wine colored lips. "We treated her for quite some time and I got to be good friends with her. She told me her husband used to hit her regularly. After she came to the hospital, somebody went and saw Amos and put him out of his misery. The more she thought about it the more she wanted to thank you and tell you she was sorry for yelling at you. When she got around to calling the precinct they told her you'd gone to New York."

"Where is she these days?"

She shook her head. "Took a train out west. She told me a good cocktail waitress could get a job anywhere."

I laughed. "That is probably true."

"So, anyway, I'd heard your name a few times and saw it in the papers other times. Patrick Moses, the detective who solved the Prostitute Murders and the Hobbs' Kidnapping. Then I heard you were living next door."

"And you decided to invite me to dinner?"

She raised her glass to me and I did the same. We clinked the glasses together. "It probably can't hurt to have a cop for a friend."

I thought of quite a few people who had been my friend and how many of them I had hurt directly or indirectly because I was a cop.

"So why did you come back?" she said.

"I was asked to help out on a case." So far the murder of the two older women had been mostly kept out of the papers, at least the similarities in their killings.

"Must be important if they wanted you to come back."

"All cases are important to somebody," I said. "So what about you? A young woman with a good job and a nice kid. No Mr. Winston?"

Her face showed no extra emotion. "William got up one day and left me. I have not heard a word since and have no idea where he is. Freddie and I had to sell the house and get this apartment. As far as

I'm concerned he is dead."

That was a pretty good way of telling me to shut up. It was getting late. I could see the skies darkening outside. "The ham was excellent. I hope you'll have me over again."

She rested her hand on top of mine again. "I would hope you would come again."

I helped her clean up and then said goodnight to Freddie. As I walked back into my own apartment it seemed to me that she knew an awful lot about me, but I seemed to know very little about her.

*****

August 8th

Keenan Coughlin was waiting for me near my desk when I arrived at the precinct the following morning. It was a little past nine. He looked neat and clean, wearing a freshly pressed light brown suit. I had on a suit, but it wasn't pressed and I didn't feel too neat. I didn't drink anymore after I left the Winston apartment, but still felt rundown.

"I have something interesting to tell you about Jack Garfield," he said.

At first the name didn't register and then I remembered that this was the cop from headquarters who was supposedly looking into my past. "I always like to listen to interesting things to start my day." I sat down at my desk; Keenan continued to stand.

"Should we just talk right here?"

I looked around. "Is it that bad?"

He shrugged and pulled up a chair close to me. He sat down. "Jack Garfield was quite the police hero during a lot of the labor rift in the city in the late eighties. He was very busy during that time, busting heads and trying to break up unions. He was an integral member of the team that dealt with the Haymarket Riot investigations. He is known as a very tough man. He is in his fifties now and does special assignments. For lack of a better term, he is a free- lancer."

"That's an interesting history lesson, Keenan, but what does any of this have to do with me?"

Keenan blushed. "Really none of it. I haven't learned anything about why he might be looking at you."

I shifted on my hard seat. "Is there more?"

"Captain Garfield, because of the nature of his assignments, has a lot of free time on his hands and also has the ability to get around the city quite easily. It seems no one keeps much of an eye on him."

"Do you mean he isn't supervised?"

"Well, he is a Captain, but no. He reports directly to the Chief. During the labor disputes he was known as quite the head basher. If he even thought someone was an anarchist, the club would come out. There seem to have been a number of complaints, but as far as I can tell, most people looked the other way."

"Sounds like a charming fellow."

"That's not all. He is a big, burly man with a ruddy complexion and a big nose. He pictures himself a ladies man, but not many of the ladies agree. From what I hear he can get a little rough with the girls if not treated right."

I was a bit surprised that I hadn't heard anything about Garfield until this date. I would check around with some of my other sources.

"That's pretty good, right?" Keenan asked. He was wearing a stupid grin.

"It's good," I said. "Doesn't tell me why he is looking at me, but it's something."

His smile went away. "I'm trying to get something on that, but no one really knows much about any investigation."

Shipley knew somehow and that bothered me. "Keep plugging. Based on what you've dug up about his past, I'm sure you'll find something."

The smile was back. "Anything else?"

"Yeah. I met a woman last night by the name of Lois Winston. She told me that her ex-husband, William, had suddenly run out on her and her son. See if you can find out anything on his disappearance."

"When did he leave?"

"I'm thinking like April."

"What does this have to do with our cases?"

I smiled. "Nothing, Keenan. This one is for my own knowledge."

He wrote down a few notes and then looked at me. "So where are we off to?"

"We are going to be off to the homes of our two victims to see if we can learn anything that the earlier investigators might have missed."

"Those guys seemed to have done a pretty thorough job."

"Seemed to have, but we have very few clues. Let's go see if maybe they missed something. See if you can secure a vehicle and I'll meet you in back."

Before I left the building, I ran into George Loftus outside of the lavatory. "Your new partner give you the lowdown on Jack Garfield?" he asked.

"He did," I said.

George lit a cigarette. "I was behind you guys and heard some of it," he said. "Coughlin got a good part of it right, but he left out a few pieces."

"Like what?"

"Garfield is an old timer. Been around a long time. He's tight with a lot of the old time politicians. As far as I know, he's tight with the aldermen down here, Coughlin and Kenna. I heard his boys handle some of the payoff collections. I've also heard Garfield doesn't mind using threats to make a little money."

I scratched my chin. "Advice, George?"

"Watch out for Garfield," he said, poking me in the chest. "And while you are at it, watch out for your new partner."

●   ●   ●

We got the landlord to let us into Grace Muldor's apartment at Twenty-Sixth and Wabash. It was a nice, neat looking little place on what seemed like a quiet little street. Everything had been cleaned up since the murder so there wasn't much to see. The landlord, a fat, bald guy named Gray, looked like he was hiding something, but a lot of people looked that way when the cops came poking around.

"You guys gonna need me much longer?" Gray asked.

"Not much," I said. "Nice little place. Did you know Mrs. Muldor?"

First he looked over at Keenan and then back at me. "Yeah, I knew her. As well as I know any tenant. Obviously, she was real quiet and she paid her rent on time, so that was never an issue. She just seemed like a sweet, little, old lady."

"Never any visitors?"

He stretched his neck to take a quick look around the place. "Twice a month a woman came in to clean the place. I told the other detectives this. I thought they wrote it down."

"Anybody else?"

"You know, those Daughters of the City came by one time, but that was over a month ago. That's about all I can remember."

"Who are the Daughters of the City?"

"They are a group of young girls, maybe thirteen and fourteen years old, who try and do good deeds throughout the neighborhood. They will visit the elderly and clean and cook for them. Maybe they'll sing some songs or read to the person. They try to help out wherever they can."

I nodded. "Sounds nice. Any idea where they are out of?"

"Sure. St. Regina's at Chicago and Milwaukee."

"That's kind of far from here."

"From what I hear, they go all over the city."

•   •   •

Keenan and I took our time on our long journey to Lincoln Park. Keenan said he would follow up on the Daughters of the City. The ride was a long one, over five miles and as we wound through the city streets, the sun peaked and the temperature rose. The humidity was stifling. Automobiles were becoming more fashionable in the city, but there weren't that many of them. Horse shit was still everywhere and the smell of it permeated our nostrils.

"So far, I can't find anything on Christian Hanson," Keenan said.

"You probably won't be able to find much on him. He's a very sly bastard. We could never find any pattern on his movements. There is none. You'll just hear he's been somewhere or that he is somewhere and you'll have to pounce."

"But it is true that he killed two of your partners?"

"I was with Sam Walker when Hanson shot him; as far as Gunter Krause, I'm not sure that Hanson did the actual killing, but Gunter went looking for him and ended up getting beaten to death."

"You know when I was assigned to you people told me that I was signing a death warrant on myself."

I looked over at the young man. He wore a look of genuine concern across his face. I thought about what George had told me, but I let it go. "Sam got killed and I was there. Gunter went looking for Hanson on his own, a stupid idea, and got killed. Hanson is a killer. That is his trade. If he sees us he will try and kill us. That is why it is important to note that if you ever lay eyes on the bastard, draw your gun and start shooting. If you should hit him and you're sure that he is dead, put one through his head anyway. The man is in concert with the devil."

Keenan's face went pale and he turned to look out of the other side of the vehicle.

• • •

We couldn't locate a landlord, or anyone for that matter, at Dorothy Casson's building. We had knocked on all of the other apartment doors with no answer. Keenan had the bright idea to try Ms. Casson's door and it opened. We walked in and looked around.

The apartment appeared to be the way it was when Ms. Casson died. In the middle of the little sitting area was a wooden kitchen chair. At the base of this chair were several strips of white bed sheets. I didn't know if these were the ones used to tie or suffocate Ms. Casson, but I picked a couple of them up. As Harold had said they were cut neatly from the whole sheet, not torn. Other than that, there wasn't much to look at. On a small table, not far from the chair, there was an open book, showing pencil sketches of plants, flowers and trees. I closed the book and noticed that it was an artist's sketch book with blank pages. I wondered if Ms. Casson had been the artist and who had been the last to look at the book. Had it been Ms. Casson or had the killer had an interest in it and left it open? I wondered if it mattered.

Convinced that we had seen whatever there was to see in the apartment, we left and closed it up. We tried the neighbor's doors again, but got no answer.

"Should we try anyone in the adjoining buildings?" Keenan

asked.

I thought for a moment, first about how damn hot it was and then about his question. "We can assume the original detectives did their work and got those answers. From what we heard no one heard or saw anything out of the ordinary the day she died."

"So what do we do?" Keenan's voice had cracked a bit, tension showing.

"That's the part of being a detective that isn't always so great. The clues don't always jump out at you and things are not as logical as Arthur Conan Doyle would like you to believe. Sometimes you just have to wait a bit."

"Wait for what?"

"Something to happen, and if my instincts are right about this killer, something will happen."

• • •

There is a saying that some things never change and I guess that is true. I had only been gone a little over seven months, but nothing at Coopers had changed. The place was still stuffy, smoke filled, with warm beer and dry chicken. It didn't help much that the temperature outside had only dipped into the low eighties by night. The bar wasn't much cooler. Most of the patrons looked tired and hot. I wasn't tired, but I was hot.

I ate my dinner alone, the dry chicken, vegetables and a potato. I drank the first beer, but only half of the second. I wouldn't say I was depressed, but it appeared that I was both alone and a little lonely. Friends I had had in the city were few to begin with and many of these were gone. Father Luigi to heart failure, Eleanor Winter to a madman and Gunter Krause to my nemesis, Christian Hanson. It wasn't that I didn't have people that I knew. Most people, I found, didn't want to get that close to me. Friends of mine seemed to end up dead. I sighed and thought of Soon Lee's, the opium den not far from where I was sitting. That sounded good, but it was also what I didn't need. Smoking to oblivion was only a temporary cure. Life was still there when you woke up.

I asked the barmaid for a whiskey and pushed the unfinished beer away from me on the table. I had promised myself to watch the drinking, but one or two wouldn't hurt anything. She brought the glass to me and asked if she should leave the bottle. I thought more than I should have and then told her to leave it.

Lieutenant Shipley had told me a couple of things that had bothered me. He had said that it was his responsibility to keep me away from alcohol and opium. I knew these bad habits of mine were hurting me, but had never considered that it might be hurting my work. That the department knew that sometimes I went a little too far did nothing to make me feel better. I sipped the bourbon.

Secondly, the word that Jack Garfield was conducting some sort of investigation into my past, particularly the two shootings. The murders of my father and Amos Stokes had been committed with the same gun, mine. The bullets taken from these two would likely match; therefore, anyone with half a brain might be able to say they that these killings were the work of one person. Why Garfield had come up with a theory that I was behind the murders was a mystery. I hated my father, no news to anyone. Amos Stokes was a fat, wife beater. His wife had helped me after she admitted to sleeping with, Frank Pelicanos, a man we were holding for allegedly killing my father, giving us the proof that he couldn't have killed him. Amos read about it in the *Tribune* and then beat Beth Stokes. I made Amos pay for his sins. Somehow Jack Garfield figured I was behind these crimes and was going to look into them. I raised the glass in a mock salute. Good luck, Jack Garfield.

My new neighbor, Lois Winston, was just as much of a mystery. She had treated Beth Stokes when Beth was at Mercy Hospital. Beth, it seems, had told her a lot about our relationship. This little fact unnerved me a bit. Beth had confided in me that she had cheated on her husband with Frank Pelicanos; she said she had been with Pelicanos the night he said he shot my father. This had been made public which led Amos to beat her. I knew she wanted to get away from Amos, but was afraid to try. I did her the honors by dispatching him. She had no idea that I was going to do this. What could she have told Lois Winston? Could she have assumed that I was her champion to do battle with Amos? There was just something about the way Lois told me the story that made me think she thought she knew a secret.

I'd have to be careful around her.

Lastly, the biggest mystery of them all, the murder of two older women in completely different sections of town. It was clear that the murders had been carried about by the same person or people. The modus operandi was the same in both case; the women had been bound and gagged, probably dying from suffocation or maybe heart attacks. Each victim had been tied to a chair using strips from their own bedsheets, neatly cut strips, not torn, as Harold Pinter pointed out.

Our clues, or lack of clues, said the killer or killers liked cake. Maybe. There were two forks by the cake, but that doesn't mean the killer or killers were the eaters. No one at either scene heard or saw anything out of the ordinary. A book of pencil sketches had been left open on a table. A group called the Daughters of the City had visited one of the victims recently. I grabbed the glass of whiskey and bolted back the last of the contents and then poured some more from the demon bottle. My actions told me how I felt. Two poor women had been cruelly murdered and we had next to nothing to tell us which direction to go in. I had half- jokingly told my young partner, Keenan Coughlin that we would have to wait for the killer to do something more before we could learn anything. I sipped the whiskey. Maybe I had been right.

Keenan had contacted the Daughters of the City and a Sister Margaret Mary from St. Regina was going to meet with us at nine o'clock the next day. I had thoughts of hitting that whiskey real hard, but both my head and my heart finally agreed. I finished my whiskey, paid my bill and headed out into the warm, muggy night to find a cab back to my apartment.

• • •

The carriage I found was an open air type so I found myself sitting in the back gazing up at the stars as the horse and driver pulled us lazily through the quiet streets. As the cab bounced along I felt myself drifting off. I wasn't drunk, but the whiskey had relaxed me quite a bit. When the driver pulled up in front of my apartment, I noticed how dark our street was. I paid him and turned towards the building.

I had taken only a few steps when the two men stepped out from the side of my building. They were both about medium height, but that was all I could tell you about them. They both wore a cloth hood over their heads, disguising them totally. They both also carried long, thick sticks. I didn't think they were there to collect for a charity.

"Good evening," I said, reaching inside my jacket for my gun.

"You lousy son of a bitch," the man to my left said.

I assumed they didn't know who I was or that I was armed. As soon as I put my hand on the gun grip someone smacked me across the back of my kidneys with a stick. The pain was excruciating. I fell quickly to my knees and fought for my breath. I had assumed wrong.

"Make sure he doesn't go for his fucking gun," one of the men said as they circled me.

"Let him try," another said.

All three got close and then they began taking turns kicking me. I covered up the best I could but my back and ribs were exposed. I took several good shots there. I coughed hard and could taste a combination of bile and blood. I had learned a valuable lesson after my last meeting with Thomas Morgan. I still kept that little knife strapped to my right ankle. I slid my hand down my leg and tried to reach for it.

One kick got me good on the side of the head and I thought for a moment how this was how I was going to die. I reached again for the knife. A light popped on in an apartment to my left in another building.

"Let's finish this bastard off," one said.

"You lousy piece of shit," said another. One more kick to my ribs.

I grabbed the knife and anticipated the sticks starting to pummel me.

"Leave him alone," I heard a woman's voice call out and then I heard the unmistakable sound of a high caliber revolver being fired.

The kicking stopped and the men all seemed to turn towards the gun. The gun was fired again and I lashed out with the knife, getting one of my attackers just above the knee. He howled like an animal and soon the three men were scampering across the street and through the side of two buildings. I laid back on the ground and let out a deep breath. I closed my eyes.

"Are you okay, Mr. Moses?" a female voice said.

"I need a doctor," I replied.

"Not much more a doctor can do that I can't," the voice said and I realized it was Lois Winston, my new neighbor.

"I need somebody."

She tried to look at me while I was lying on the ground, but it was too dark. "Let's see if we can get you upstairs to my apartment. Can you stand?"

I hurt in several spots, but I didn't think there was anything terribly wrong with me. I tried to stand and Lois got her arm under my arm and helped me to stand. I was a little woozy, but didn't feel like I was going to faint.

"You okay?" she asked.

"I think so."

"Let's get upstairs and take a look."

She helped me to the apartment door and up the stairs to the second floor. I wasn't great, but I wasn't dying. She got me into her apartment and onto a chair in the kitchen. She turned the light on and started to examine my head and face. I could see she was dressed in her bed clothes and robe. It didn't mean she was any less pretty, but I wasn't in much of a mood to be romantic.

"You didn't bother to get dressed?" I asked.

"You would have been dead if I had waited too much longer."

"You heard what was going on?"

"Not at all. I looked out the window at the moment your carriage pulled up and saw them attack. I grabbed my gun and got down the stairs as fast as I could."

"Well, I'm glad you did."

She wet a rag and applied it to several places on my head where I had been kicked. She didn't come away with any blood. She then had me take off my suit jacket and shirt and examined my back. I heard her mumble a few times and felt her fingers probing what were now good sized bruises. That didn't feel too good.

"Take a deep breath and let the air out."

I did as I was told.

"Any pain?"

"Not too bad I said."

"You're not lying, are you?"

"Would I lie?"

She didn't smile, but kept on looking and probing. "Doesn't look too bad. Let me grab a couple of pills."

She left the room for a minute and returned with a small vile that contained some white tablets. She gave me a couple with a glass of water. "Pain pills," she said.

I took the pills and swallowed. Between Lois and Pinter, pills were helping me get along. The pills left a slight acidic taste on my tongue.

"I think you are going to be fine," she said. "It looks like you took some pretty good rib and kidney shots, but nothing major happened. If you see blood in your urine, we may have to take you in, but I think you're going to make it."

"Is that your professional opinion?"

"Are you always such a smart mouth?"

"I stabbed one of them in the leg with a knife. I think I got him right above the knee. I stuck it in pretty good."

She nodded. "If he gets treatment at Mercy, maybe I can figure out who did this to you."

"That's my job," I said.

"It doesn't hurt to look and ask around."

I laughed. "Where'd you get the gun?"

"Present from an old friend. He taught me how to shoot it and figured it might be a good idea for a woman in the city to be protected."

"Well, it sure worked at protecting me."

• • •

Even though I was tired and banged up and bruised, I had a surge of adrenaline from the fight and I had trouble sleeping. My lower back near my kidneys and my ribs ached a bit, but not too bad. There was no blood in my urine so I felt good knowing that nothing had been too badly damaged. In the mirror, I could see a nice bruise under my left eye and a scrape on my chin. Behind my right ear there was a lump and when I touched it I came away with some dried blood. I'd been in worse shape before, but still got that feeling that this was a hell of a way to make a living. If you weren't fighting for your life or getting beat up something would torment you mentally. I kept thinking of opium, but held off that demon for a while.

Something about what Lois Winston had told me stuck in my head and made me think. She said she had just happened to look out of her window as the attack began. I was grateful for that, but found it a little coincidental. The night had been extremely quiet and there was no cause for her to look out the window. For some reason I found it more plausible that she was waiting for me to come home. Why I do not know, but that made more sense. I shook my head to rid that thought and sat in a cushioned chair to try and sleep. Lying down had been a little too painful.

Thoughts of who had just tried to beat me, Lois Winston, Jack Garfield, Christian Hanson and two murdered old women kept me awake for a good while, but sometime during the warm night, I drifted off.

*****

August 9th

My new faithful companion, Keenan Coughlin, was right on time, pounding on my apartment door at eight-thirty the next morning. He looked very bright and cheery, dressed in a nice navy, pinstripe suit. "Good morning, Patrick!" he said as he stepped into my unit and then got a good look at me. "Oh, my god! What happened?"

"I fell on my way home," I said.

"Did you fall off of a cliff?"

"No. Actually I was rather well behaved, only two glasses of whiskey. When I got home, a group of three thugs gave me a homecoming of sorts. I was greeted with salutations such as 'you son of a bitch' and 'you piece of shit'."

"So they know you?" Keenan said with a sly smile.

I returned the smile and nodded. "Very good. As a matter of fact, I think they did know me. Thankfully, my new neighbor Lois Winston showed up with her Colt revolver or I might not be here. She managed to scare them away before things got too far out of hand. I also stabbed one of the ruffians in the leg with a four inch blade. I'm pretty sure I got him with at least three of those inches, right above the knee. Mrs. Winston, a nurse at Mercy, said she would inquire today about anyone being treated for a knife wound."

"This is the same woman who you wanted me to check out about her missing husband?"

"One and the same."

"She filed a report in late March of this year that her husband was gone, missing according to her. According to the report, she said he didn't return from work one night and had never come back. He'd been gone about a week."

"She waited a week to report him missing?"

"That's what the report says."

"They had not fought or nothing out of the ordinary precipitated this disappearance?"

Keenan shook his head. "The report was prepared by a detective at the Central Station where she went to file. Unfortunately the cop only recorded the bare facts. There weren't many inquisitive questions asked."

I wondered for a moment. Lois Winston was an attractive woman. Freddie, her son, seemed like a great little kid. What makes her husband, or any man for that matter, just up and leave. There are a number of possible reasons, another woman, financial or possibly just mental illness, but Lois had said he had just left with her having no clue as to why. This made so little sense it was staggering.

"So who do you think attacked you?" Keenan asked.

I had thought a bit in this during my rough night of sleep. My first guess was that Hanson had learned I was back in town and had sent a welcoming party. This was the only thing that made any sense, but for some reason telling Keenan didn't seem like the best thing to do. "I really don't have any idea."

I don't know that he believed me or didn't, but there was no response on that topic.

"We should be going if we are going to be on time for our meeting with Sister Margaret Mary," Keenan said.

"The Daughters of the City."

"A group that goes around the city helping those in need in various ways."

'Well, let's see if they can help us figure out who suffocated two old women."

Keenan had commandeered a carriage and had it wait for us until we got downstairs. It was just past eight-thirty and it was already beastly hot with horrible humidity. At least this little section of the city didn't stink so badly. When we were in the cab an on our way to the north, Keenan took a photograph out of his suit jacket pocket. He showed it to me.

The young lady was attractive with a little pug nose, dimpled cheeks and a head full of tight curls. "Your sister, I assume?"

He laughed. "Lorrabelle Andrews, Captain Andrews' daughter. We are to be married at the end of October." He wore a big smile.

I heard what he said and I smiled, but it was forced. I hadn't done too well with my married partners. Both Gunter and Sam Walker had been married and both had kids. Both were now dead. I felt a bolt of anxiety rush up the back of my neck and across my head.

"Nothing more to say?" Keenan asked.

"Congratulations," I said. "She looks like a lovely girl."

• • • •

St. Regina was a newer parish in the Western part of the city located on Chicago Avenue. In comparison to Holy Trinity where I was raised it was like a baby, around only ten years or so. When I first asked about it the term "progressive" had been used. I wasn't sure of the exact definition for that term with respect to a parish, but my thought was it meant going forward. If that was true, that was a good idea when dealing with children. I just wondered what the church thought of the term.

My memory from Holy Trinity was that all of the nuns and priests were old. When I was a small boy they all seemed to be over a hundred years old. The nuns were always bent over and ancient looking; the priests, archaic, and walking about on failing legs. Neither species smiled very much. As I got older, my appreciation for both went way up.

Sister Margaret Mary was in charge of the school that was attached to the parish church. She was a younger nun and might have actually been attractive without the habit. As it was, she wore the same tough look I was used to from the sisters of my past.

"How may I help you two officers this morning?" We were in her small office and she had the look of someone who was very busy.

"It's detectives, sister," Keenan said.

She smiled. "Sorry, detectives."

"You run a program out of the parish called the Daughters of the City?" I asked.

She was standing behind her desk and now she strode out to the front of it where we were standing. She was very short, barely breaking five feet. I wondered how she could be comfortable in the full habit that she wore on this hot morning. "We do," she said. "Is there some sort of a problem with the program?"

"Not the program itself," I said. "We are interested in some of the people that your program visited."

She eyed me closely for the first time. The side of the face that she could see from where she was standing sprouted the biggest bruise. She didn't respond to my question right away. When she realized that my injuries were not life threatening she responded. "The program has been going for three years now. The list of people that we help out is getting rather long."

"We don't need to see the entire list," Keenan said. "We are actually only inquiring about two of the people who might be your list."

Sister Margaret Mary moved back to her side of the desk and opened one of the drawers. She took out a thick ledger. "Who are the two people that you are inquiring about?"

"Grace Muldor and Dorothy Casson."

I could see that the ledger was alphabetized and Sister Margaret flipped to the C's first. She scrolled down the page, using her finger to guide her. "Ah, yes. We saw Mrs. Casson on July twentieth. The girls went with a group led by Sister Francis."

"And Mrs. Muldor?" Keenan persisted.

She flipped through the pages some more and then ran her fingers down first one and then another page. "Mrs. Grace Muldor. The girls saw her on July seventh; they were led by Sister Theresa."

Two victims both visited by the Daughters of the City. "What was the nature of the visits?" I asked.

She closed the ledger and peered at me. "These were elderly ladies. We help them in any way we can. Sometimes cleaning, laundry, cooking a meal or maybe even writing a letter. The girls are always strictly supervised. Was there some sort of complaint?"

"No complaints," I said. "Nothing was wrong with anything to do with your visits."

Her look told us we were totally confusing her.

"I'm sorry to say, Sister, but both of these women were murdered within weeks of your visits to see them. We learned that your group had made a visit to one of them and since we have absolutely no leads in the case we thought we would pay a visit."

"But you said nothing had occurred during our visits."

"That is correct, but maybe these visits gave someone the idea that these two women lived by themselves and would be totally vulnerable. I realize that this idea may be a little farfetched, but we have to check every lead."

"So you are asking me to come up with a list of every person, other than the girls, who might have knowledge of where the trips were going, someone who might use that knowledge later?"

"I think that would be of great use to us."

"I don't think that is necessary," she said smartly.

I swallowed hard and I heard Keenan gasp a bit. "I'm sorry," I said.

"No list is necessary. The person you seek is our carriage driver, Mr. Duvall. He is a man of questionable character and a past police record. I was hesitant to bring him on, but one of the local ward bosses asked a favor of Father Grimley and Duvall was hired."

"You're certain that this is our man?" I asked. I was not convinced.

"If he is not then I will prepare your list immediately," she said, closing her ledger with a snap.

"Then, if you will tell us where we can find him, we will pay Mr. Duvall a visit."

• • •

The apartment building that Roger Duvall lived in was a mile west of St. Regina. We got there as quickly as we could, but found no one home.

"Should we ask around?" Keenan asked.

"No. We can return later. I'm not so sure Duvall is our man. I don't think we have to pursue him all over the city at this time."

• • •

When we returned to the precinct I was hailed by Charlie Coogan, the sergeant that was manning the front desk that morning. Coogan was an older cop with gray hair and bushy eyebrows and mustache. He had a twinkle in his eye and a good sense of humor which always gave you the impression he was in a good mood. Many said his attitude came from the small flask he kept in his inside breast pocket. The nips of whiskey he took brought the glow to his cheeks and the enhancement of his mood.

"Moses, a cop from headquarters stopped by early this morning and left you this envelope." Charlie handed me a regular white envelope.

"Any idea what it is?"

He shrugged. "It ain't ten grand because it's pretty thin."

I walked a few steps away and opened the envelope. There was a short note, neatly written on a small card: "Meet me at Southside Park, one PM. Captain Garfield."

It wasn't much of a request. Actually it was more of a demand. Also included in the envelope was a ticket to today's baseball game between the Detroit Tigers and the Chicago White Sox. I never cared much for baseball. I never played as a boy. I found it slow paced and a bit boring. I doubted I was being asked by a cop who was investigating me for two homicides to a game for its enjoyment. The only reason I decided at that moment to accept the invitation was to find out exactly what Jack Garfield wanted from me.

The newest rendition of Southside Park was located on Thirty-Ninth Street, not too far from the Levee. It was another warm day and I watched as several thousand people flowed into the park for the game. I was told that the ticket that I held was for a seat in the third row just behind home plate. I ambled down the stairs towards the seat. The game had already begun.

When I got to my seat, I found it was an open one on the aisle. In the seat next to mine was an older man, barrel-chested, ruddy faced with an even bushier mustache than Charlie Coogan. The most distinguishing feature about this fellow was his coal black eye balls. When I walked up to the row the two eyes fixed onto my face.

"Ah, Moses," a gravelly voice said. "I'm glad you could make it."

I took the empty seat. "Captain Garfield, I presume?"

He laughed. "You presume correctly."

There was suddenly a loud groan from the crowd and I looked towards the batter's box; we were that close. A tough-looking, left-handed batter was getting ready to take his swings for the Tigers.

"Follow baseball much, Moses?" Garfield asked.

"Not much," I admitted.

"This son of a bitch batting is Ty Cobb, the Tiger's best hitter. Mark my words that he will be a great player for some time. I watch a lot of games and this boy is a good one. Funny thing is, his daddy was a Georgia state senator. I say was because his wife shot him dead while he was snooping around outside her window after he suspected her of cheating on him. The courts did not find her guilty when she said she thought he was a prowler."

There was a loud crack of the bat, and the crowd groaned as Cobb drove a ball between the right and center fielder. Cobb took off fast and had to slide into second base in a cloud of dust to beat the fielder's throw.

"Damn, that boy can hit," Garfield said.

He looked good to me, too. I'd seen him bat once and he had one hit. "I'm pretty sure, Captain, that you didn't invite me out here to watch the game."

It was pretty damn hot out again and Garfield wiped his sweaty forehead with the sleeve of his suit coat. He continued to look straight ahead as the next Tiger hitter got ready to bat. "We don't have to jump right ahead and talk business. It's okay to relax a bit, maybe enjoy a beer."

"I'm currently trying to figure out the murders of two elderly women. I don't have a lot of time to relax, and, Captain, I find baseball to be boring."

He turned to look in my direction. "You lose some sort of fist fight?"

"Some drunk decided he thought I was trying to talk with his girl and caught me with a cheap shot."

He pointed at the two obviously different bruises on my face. "One punch did a lot of damage."

"Hurt like hell, too," I said.

He nodded. "You'll need to be careful now that you are back in the Levee. I hear quite a bit of people aren't all that fond of you. You seem to have a way, Moses, of not making friends wherever you go."

"I wasn't aware of my immense unpopularity, but thank you for the warning."

The Tiger batter hit a soft pop fly to the left side of the infield where the shortstop made an easy catch. Ty Cobb stood patiently at second.

Garfield spoke to me again. This time his voice was much lower. "Within a matter of a few weeks before your departure to New York there were two murders committed near the Levee which have raised some suspicions."

"Just two?" I asked.

"Two that seem eerily similar. One is that of your father; the other was Amos Stokes. It appears that both men were shot at close range with a caliber of bullet that matches those from guns issued to members of our department."

I heard the crowd rise from their seats and I did as well. Ty Cobb was attempting to steal third. The catcher's throw seemed to beat him to the base, but Cobb slid in, spikes very high, and collided violently with the third baseman. The baseman clearly had the ball, but when Cobb's spikes sliced his arms the ball fell free and Cobb was safe. He stood on the base dusting himself off and then spat a large wad of tobacco refuse near the fielder who was still kneeling in the dirt and examining his fresh wounds.

"That man plays as if he were possessed," Garfield said.

"Seems a bit out of line for baseball."

"Anyway," Garfield continued, "there are a few that suggest you weren't always on the best of terms with your father. There are also a few that say that after Amos Stokes beat his wife, Beth, a witness of yours, that you stepped up and enacted revenge for her. Obviously, Moses, these are most serious charges. It is my intention to seek as much evidence as I can to put these rumors to bed."

"So you are acting in my behalf?"

He put up one finger to quiet me. "I am acting on behalf of the department and I am acting on behalf of those two murdered men. Hopefully, these rumors are silly and fruitless. Then you will have no problem. Hopefully I do not find out that you hated your father so much and that you were so angry with Amos Stokes for what he did to his wife that you decided to kill both of them. If that is the case, I can only recommend prosecution."

He had turned his attention back to the game and I knew our conversation was over. I sat there a few minutes watching Garfield study the game. Like I said, baseball bores me. "Enjoy the rest of the game, Captain." I got up and left the park.

• • •

We returned to Roger Duvall's apartment around four-thirty in the afternoon. The damn heat was so oppressive and consistent, I think I was getting used to it. My shirt, under my suit coat, was getting soaked. I looked over at Keenan. He seemed cooler than I. It made me wonder how much different one could feel in certain situations. That made me wonder how someone could murder two old women for seemingly no other reason than to kill them. Baffling, the human being.

"I got a line on your friend, Christian Hanson," Keenan said suddenly.

I immediately popped out of my contemplation of humans. "What kind of a line?"

"There was a fight in a tavern over in Pilsen. From what I hear, two men were arguing and a few punches were thrown. One man, big guy, blonde hair parted down the middle, pulled a knife. That stopped the fight until this blonde guy, with a couple of friends, were able to make their way out of the bar."

Hanson and bar fights were getting to be a common theme. "You say they were arguing? Hanson is a mute." I thought of the dream where he talked to me.

"That's the story I got, Patrick. Some arguing, a fight broke out and this guy, maybe Hanson, yanked a knife and that was it."

I nodded. "Pilsen. Not too far from us."

"You said his Chicago roots were in this area."

"At least south of the river. Probably anywhere near the underbelly."

"That could be anywhere," Keenan said.

Keenan pounded on Roger Duvall's first floor apartment door. There was no answer so Keenan pounded loudly again.

"Who the fuck is it and what's your problem?" said a voice from behind the door. It was flung open and there stood a man of medium height, slight build, dirty undershirt and disheveled hair. His face and eyes told the story better. He'd been drinking.

Keenan flashed his badge. "You Roger Duvall?"

Duvall squinted at the badge. "That's who I am."

"Can we come in and have a word?" Keenan asked.

"You're the police," Duvall slurred. "Don't think I can say no."

Duvall let us into the place which was a little flat with one large room, a kitchen area and a bathroom to the rear. The place had the smell of body odor, old beer and spent cigarettes. It also was very dark.

"Mind if I use the bathroom before we talk?" Duvall asked.

"Go ahead," Keenan said. I was busy scanning the room for anything of importance, but it was mostly disorganized garbage.

I happened to focus on Duvall as he made his way down the short hall past the kitchen. He stopped by the bathroom door and looked back at me. Even in the gloomy light I could see the look on his face. "Keenan!" I yelled.

Just as I yelled Duvall made a quick turn and was pushing open an outside door which was just across from the bathroom. He may have been on his way to a good drunk, but he was quickly out that door and on his way through the yard to the alley in back of the building.

Keenan, younger than me and in much better physical condition, was down the hall and out the door as soon as I yelled. I followed and stepped into the glaring sun. I saw Duvall glance off a garbage can, stumble and then start down the alley. Keenan was closing ground as I pulled up to the alley. The chase wasn't all that exciting. Keenan quickly caught him from behind, knocked him down and had his hands cuffed behind him. Duvall immediately curled himself into a ball in the dirt.

"Don't hit me. I didn't mean to do it. Just don't hit me," Duvall squealed.

"Shut up," Keenan said as I came up to them. He looked at me.

"He's confessing to something already."

I knelt down by Duvall and it was clear that he had started to cry. I reached out and touched his arm and he flinched. "Calm down," I said. "We're not going to hit you."

"Those last cops hit me," he said.

I looked at Keenan. We both had no idea what he was talking about. "Why don't you tell us what you didn't mean to do?"

He had wound himself into such a tight ball he looked like any further movement might make him snap a body part. His eyes were closed as he clearly expected to be pummeled.

"Mr. Duvall," I said, "we are going to help you to your feet. We then want you to answer some questions for us. If you cooperate things will go well. If you don't we will take you into the precinct where it might not be as pleasant."

He slowly opened his eyes and looked at us. There were tears running from his eyes and snot running from his nose. Keenan knelt and wiped his face clean with a handkerchief.

"Do you understand?" I said.

"Yes," he said meekly.

We took the cuffs off of him and got him back into his small apartment. Keenan got him a drink of water. He was sweating profusely and was covered with dirt and bits of grass from his tumble on the ground. His eyes said that he didn't believe us. They darted back and forth between us; he still thought we were going to beat him up. He drank a bit of the water and took a deep breath, sighing loudly.

"We are not going to beat you up," I said.

He still looked like a wild animal that we had just trapped. "Those other two cops, they beat me when I messed up. I didn't want to do it. I'm sorry."

These responses didn't seem to have much to do with the investigation of the two murdered women. "How long have you been a driver for St. Regina?" I asked.

He looked at me as if he didn't understand the question. "St. Regina?"

I wanted to beat him to speed things up, but he seemed legitimately confused. "Yeah, the parish on Chicago. You know, Sister

Margaret Mary."

He took another drink. "Yeah, I know St. Regina and the sister. What's that got to do with the cops?"

"Probably nothing", I said.

"Probably nothing," he said slowly. "I thought those two cops were going to kill me last time."

It was time to clear one problem up before pursuing another. "Why don't you tell us what you are sorry for that you didn't want to do? The thing the cops beat you up for?"

It looked like he was calming down. He was still sweating, but his breathing was coming a little easier. "It's the Bower's Meats thing. I haul some meat for them, stuff that they've cleaned up, down to the local markets. I'm always back there in the loading area. There is so much meat back there, steaks and chops and roasts. I always load my cab with the right orders and then I always take more. The extra that I take goes to these two cops. I'm not sure what happens after I give it to them."

"So you missed a delivery date and these two cops paid you a visit?"

He nodded. "I always run deliveries for Bower's on Wednesdays. I just didn't want to steal anymore from them. They are nice people. I was trying to stop." Tears started to form in his eyes.

"They pay you for anything that you steal?"

"No." He sniffled a few times.

"Then what's in this little game for you?" I asked.

Again his eyes darted around the room. He was clearly nervous about the secret he was about to share with us. "As long as I keep up the stealing, they won't go to Sister Margaret Mary about my past police record."

Sister Margaret had told us about his record. Maybe there was something really awful in it. "What's in that record?"

He shrugged. "A couple of petty thefts and a robbery. Not really that much."

I took a step forward and he backed away. "Is that all?"

"I got in trouble once when they say I took advantage of a younger girl. I shouldn't have done it, but she wasn't right in the head. I was in for about a month for that."

I could see where the specifics of this crime would upset Sister Margaret. "What about what you do for St. Regina?"

"I only work for them when they need me. It's not always steady. Most of the time it's taking the Daughters of the City around to sites."

"What does that entail?"

"Not a whole lot. They tell me where to take a group of girls and then I take them. I wait around with the wagon until they return and then I bring them back to St. Regina."

"You ever see or know who the girls are providing a service for?"

"The people, no. I just know the location address and that's where I go. Whoever is leading the group that day takes the girls into the location. I don't have anything to do with that."

"Ever hear the name Grace Muldor or Dorothy Casson?"

Duvall scrunched his yes together like he was thinking really hard. "I can't say that I have."

"Do you have any means of conveyance?"

"What the hell is that?"

"Do you own a wagon or carriage?"

"Oh, no. I get to St. Regina or Bower's on the electric car. It takes up a lot of what I earn."

I nodded. "Anything, Keenan?"

"The two cops that beat you. What were their names?"

He looked back at me. "Answer him," I said.

"I don't know. They came to see me, showed their badges and told me how the plan was going to work. Two big, scary fellows. I never got their names."

"Come on," Keenan pressed. "You've got to know their names."

"Forget it," I said quickly.

"What? Patrick?" Keenan protested.

I told Duvall that I was sorry about his predicament with the two cops. I also told him he'd better keep a clean slate or I would come visit him again and let Sister Margaret know what I had found. He nodded several times and seem to understand.

"Why didn't you want the two cop's names?" Keenan asked. We were in a cab on the way back towards the Levee.

"It's not our fight," I said. "If it's just these two cops boosting DuVall, I don't give a shit."

Keenan turned to look out the other side of the carriage. I'm sure he didn't think this was the right way to uphold justice, but I really didn't care.

• • •

Freddie Winston was on the front porch when I got home from my dinner at Cooper's. It was not quite eight o'clock, but the light was sifting out of the day. Summer was coming to a close and soon the days would shorten. As I got close, I saw that Freddie was busy playing a game of jacks. He had his head down and barely heard or saw me walk up to the building.

"You winning, Freddie?" I asked.

He looked up at me and smiled. "Only playing by myself. Tommy Martin always seems to beat me so I thought I'd better practice."

Reminded me of my early days at Holy Trinity, getting beat up a lot. That didn't stop until I started working at being a boxer. "Practice will make you better," I said. "What are you doing out here on the stoop by yourself?"

"My mom asked me to wait out here for you until you got home as long as it wasn't too late. She wants you to come up for a piece of pie."

"Pie?"

"It's apple. I already had mine, but mom didn't have hers' yet. She was waiting for you and she made some coffee."

I looked at Freddie, mom's little lookout. "I could use a piece of pie."

Lois Winston was still wearing her nurse's uniform minus the little hat when I entered their apartment. She smiled broadly as Freddie led me into the kitchen. Fresh brewed coffee and apple pie were all that I could smell.

"Ah, Detective Moses. So glad that you could make it."

"How could I resist pie and coffee with a lovely lady?"

She gave me a bit of a smirk as I sat down at the table. She quickly cut two pieces of pie and poured two cups of coffee. She offered neither cream nor sugar. She told Freddie to start getting ready for bed as she took the chair across from me. "Your face doesn't look too bad."

"It would have been a lot worse if you hadn't shown up." I tasted the pie. It was delicious. "This is great. Did you make it?"

She laughed. "I can cook a bit, but pies aren't on the list. I got it at a little bakery near the hospital."

The coffee was good, too, hot and soothing as I drank it. "This really is a treat."

She gave me another stern look. I didn't know what to make of her.

"The man you stabbed last night," she said.

"You mean one of my attackers? It wasn't just some man that I stabbed."

"Of course. I didn't mean to sound flippant. Anyway, he showed up later at the hospital seeking treatment."

I looked up, half a piece of pie crammed in my mouth. "Anybody call the cops?"

"Didn't need to."

I swallowed and sipped some coffee. "There were police officers there?"

"No. The man that was stabbed and the man that brought him in were police officers. They said he had been stabbed by a drunk in the bar. That's what Marie told me. Anyway, no one would have thought that two police officers were on the wrong end of a crime. The cop with the knife wound was treated and let go. It took about twelve stitches to close up the wound."

Small consolation, I thought, for getting your head and kidneys kicked in. "I don't suppose any of the staff at Mercy happened to get the poor, injured police officer's name?"

Again that look. "You shouldn't be so sarcastic". She took a piece of paper out of the pocket of her nurse's dress and opened it up. "Daniel Bergman. Works out of police headquarters as a Special Investigator."

I sat back in the chair and got some quick understanding. My meeting with Jack Garfield at the ballgame hadn't been my introduction to his unit of Special Investigations, but why would he send three of his goons to beat me? Maybe he hadn't sent them, but then why had they come?

"Are you okay, Detective Moses? You looked a little distant for a moment."

Suddenly I had little appetite left for my pie and the coffee tasted bitter. My ribs hurt and I could feel the two bruises on my face. "I'm okay," I said. "A bit shocked that the people that beat me were cops. That's all."

Now Lois wore a worried look. "Who can you go to within the department and tell them this kind of story? It's not like you can walk into administration and tell them that three police officers attacked you."

"It's not like that at all," I said, wanting to end the conversation. "Lois, I don't mean to get personal, but after you reported your husband missing did the police ever get back to you?"

"That's a sudden shift in conversation. It's a bit odd."

"Not so odd. When you said he had just disappeared, I checked. You filed a missing person's report. I was just curious about what was found, if anything."

She sighed. "I called and stopped by the division doing the investigation several times. They always told me that they had nothing and would let me know when they did. This went on for a while. After about a month, a detective came by and told me they had no idea where William had gone. Vanished, they said."

"Vanished?"

"Into thin air."

I felt the tension building at my temples. Little flashing lights appeared before my eyes. Lois Winston became blurry. A wave of nausea swept over me. I took two deep breaths and felt a little better. It was time to go.

"You don't look all that well, Detective Moses."

"It's been a tough week," I said.

•   •   •

Lois saw me to the door and we said goodnight. Back in my own apartment, I sat down and placed a cold rag across my forehead. I felt dizzy, but maybe it was only the thoughts that swirled through my head. Why had Jack Garfield or someone else sent those thugs to beat me? What the hell had happened to William Winston? Was Christian Hanson out there somewhere? Lastly, the only question I was supposed to be concerned with, who had murdered those two old women?

*****

August 10th

I had said we might need something to happen in order for us to get our next clues. Well, something happened. The victim's name was Agnes Gilford, age eighty-four. Her home was located at Thirty-Fourth and Illinois. The rest of her family had gone away to the east coast; they had been gone three weeks. Agnes had not wanted to make the trip. Now she was tied to a chair in her expansive living room with her own bedsheets. She had been blindfolded and her mouth had also been stuffed with pieces of her pillows.

There was a little twist in this case. Hanging from a gaudy chandelier, in plain sight of Agnes, assuming she could see it when the act was committed, was a little cat. Again, bedsheet strips were the culprit. Several strips had been tied together and wrapped tightly around the poor animal's neck. The cat was hanging straight down, as dead as Agnes.

One of the neighbors hadn't seen Agnes in a couple of days. She had called the precinct and since this location was close by we came right over

"I'd say two or three days at most," Harold Pinter said.

"The neighbor said she last saw Agnes on Thursday so maybe she was killed on Friday," I said.

"That seems to fit the time frame," Harold said.

Keenan was standing nearby. He wasn't saying much and his skin was a very pale color. "You feeling okay, Keenan? I asked.

He nodded. "I've seen dead bodies before," he said slowly. "I've just never seen one where it appears that murder was the only reason for the person dying. This is no crime of passion. There doesn't appear to be any burglary signs. This poor woman was killed because somebody wanted to torture her and watch her die."

Harold looked at me and lowered his eyes to the floor. I took a deep breath. "It's important for you to know that we live in a world of mostly good, but evil is always here. Sometimes in the Levee we get more of the evil than other people. Our job is to get rid of as much evil as we can."

"Yeah, okay, I understand that, but this is just bullshit."

That was a good way to describe what we had. Another body and this time the victim's cat. No signs of forced entry. No signs that the place had been rifled. Everything pointed to the fact that Agnes had let her killer or killers into the house.

"Do you think they made her watch while they killed her cat?" Keenan asked. He didn't look any better and I could tell he was struggling with all of this.

I looked up at the poor cat. Why else hang it right in front of her? "That seems logical," I said.

"Son of a bitch, fucking bastards," Keenan said as he turned away and walked to the front windows where all the shades were drawn.

"Patrick, without examining the body more thoroughly this looks like a copy of the first two. This poor woman either suffocated or had a heart attack. I hope for her sake she died quickly and didn't have to endure the sight of them hanging her cat. I really won't know more until the coroner's done with her," Harold said.

I nodded. "Okay. There doesn't appear to be a lot more here to look at. Might as well let the coroner's people in to cart her away."

As I said that, Riley O'Donnell and George Loftus came out of a hall that led to the back of the house. Riley was smoking up a storm; he never was big on the murder scenes. Loftus looked his usual cool self. "You might want to see this," he said, pointing towards the rear of the house. I had dispatched them to see if they could find anything unusual.

Harold and I started out to follow the two down the hall. I turned back and called to Keenan to come along. He turned towards me and I could tell he was crying. He shook his head and I nodded. I took off down the hall.

Towards the back of the house was a kitchen that you could have put my entire apartment into. Not only was it big, but everything in it was modern and shiny. Pots and pans hanging from the walls gleamed in the light. All counter space was spotless except where George Loftus was standing. On the counter to the left of George was a cut glass dish with a matching lid. Under the lid I could see maybe a half dozen cookies. Around the dish were crumbs and several broken cookie pieces.

"First cake and now cookies," Loftus said. "Our killer likes his sweets."

"Or killers," I said, remembering the two forks.

"Maybe," George said. "Regardless, he or they, kills the poor woman and then has a treat."

Riley coughed, a rough smoker's hack. "So now we are looking for suspects that like cake and cookies?"

I laughed. "I like cake and cookies."

"Then you are a suspect," Riley said.

"It doesn't help much," George conceded.

I looked around the nearly spotless kitchen. In this room and in the rest of the house there wasn't much to see. Strips of the victim's bedsheets and pillow stuffing were used to tie and suffocate the poor woman to death. Nothing else seemed out of place. "We'd better talk to the neighbor lady," I said.

"And Sister Margaret," Keenan said from the corner of the room. He wasn't crying any longer, but his eyes were red. "We need to see if Ms. Gilford was one of the women that the Daughters of the City had paid a visit to."

"We will do that," I said.

"I will let you know what the coroner finds as soon as I hear," Harold said.

"Me and George are going to hang around some of the bakeries in the area to see if we see any kind of suspicious bastards," Riley said.

We all laughed, even Keenan. Sometimes humor rears its head at the oddest times, even a murder scene.

• • •

The neighbor who found who found Agnes Gilford was named Anne Murphy. I didn't think she was as old as Agnes had been, but she couldn't have been too far behind. She had returned to her own house across the street and was sitting in her living room. Her husband had brought her a cup of tea and was sitting with her. Anne had white hair and red eyes. Her hands were holding a wet handkerchief and were resting in her lap. She was staring straight ahead when Keenan and I walked into the room.

"Would you like something to drink officers?" Mr. Murphy said. He was a big man, with a big gut. His eyes were fine, but his cheeks and nose had the red glow of a heavy drinker.

"No, that's fine," I said. "We'd just like to ask Mrs. Murphy a few questions."

"Is it alright if the officers ask you a couple of questions, Annie?" he asked.

She sniffled a bit and wiped her nose. Then she nodded slowly.

I looked at Keenan. He seemed to be getting back to normal.

"Mrs. Murphy," I said, "can you remember the last time you saw Mrs. Gilford?"

She wiped at a couple of rolling tears and returned her hands to her lap. "At least four days ago. Maybe Thursday. She was out in her front yard, pulling a few weeds. I would see her out there a couple of times a week."

"I see. Why did you walk over today?"

"I don't know why," she said, sobbing a bit. "I hadn't seen Agnes in a while and I just thought I'd check. I knew her family was out of town. I knocked on the door, but there was no answer. I tried the knob and it opened right away. I took a few steps into the house and I saw her and her cat. Most awful thing I've ever seen."

She was crying more now and her husband patted her arm. Again she wiped away tears with the handkerchief.

"This question is for both of you. Have either of you seen anyone around the Gilford house leading up to the last time you saw her? Somebody a little unusual?"

"Not really," Mr. Murphy said. "We talked about it. The only one I saw was the dairy delivery man. I'm pretty sure that I saw him early Friday morning. I saw his wagon and then I saw him up on the porch with his delivery."

Keenan was taking notes. "What time was that, sir?" he asked.

"I usually walk out to get my newspaper around seven so it would have been around then," Murphy said.

"And that's it?" I asked.

A few muffled sobs came out of Anne. "That Burke boy. I see him wondering around between the houses over there sometimes."

"Who is he?"

"James Burke," Mr. Murphy said. "Judge Burke's kid. You see him just walking about in the back of the houses, smoking cigarettes. I don't think he's any trouble, but I guess you never know."

I didn't know who Judge Burke was, but I would. I would also get to know his son. "When was the last time either one of you saw James Burke lurking around."

Anne Murphy looked up at me. "It happens so often that I don't pay that much attention to it anymore."

"But maybe between Thursday and today?"

"I would think that would be possible. I actually think it was Friday in the early afternoon."

* * *

Once Agnes Gilford's body was removed from her house, along with her cat, we were able to return to the precinct. We found the name of the dairy, Homeland Dairy, and that would be an afternoon stop. We had also gone by the Burke's house but no one was home. They would also get a visit in the afternoon. When we got back we were immediately summoned into Lieutenant Shipley's office. He looked unnerved.

"What can you tell me about the Agnes Gilford murder?" he blurted.

"Not very much," I said. "She was killed in the same fashion as the first two women, tied up with bedsheets and suffocated. The killer also hung her cat."

"Suspects?"

"None really unless you count the neighbor boy who wanders around smoking behind her house and maybe the dairy delivery man.

Other than that, nothing."

He slammed his hand down sharply on his desk. "How can three older women get murdered in their own homes and nobody hears or sees anything?"

I didn't have an answer so I didn't speak.

"Well, we have another problem," Shipley said. "Mrs. Agnes Gilford is the mother of Hamilton Gilford who happens to be the Chief Counsel for the city. I was told that the mayor was going to contact him on the Jersey shore right after lunch. Obviously, this will bring a tremendous amount of pressure from City Hall on us to solve this case."

"This case or all three cases?" I said.

"You know what I mean, Moses," he said. "What the hell happened to your face?"

I wanted to tell him about my meeting with the thugs and then the baseball game with Jack Garfield, but I didn't. I needed to find out exactly what was going on before I said anything to anyone. "I ran into my door in the dark."

He shook his head. "Get me some suspects," he said.

• • •

The visit to Homeland Dairy didn't tell us much. The delivery man was a short, fat guy named Morgan Nelson. He had made his delivery at seven-nineteen in the morning on Friday. Agnes Gilford had signed for it. Nelson said she looked fine when he saw her. He then showed us time receipts for all the other deliveries that morning. Most were within ten or fifteen minutes of each other. He had signed out back at the dairy at five-thirty in the evening. If Agnes had been killed during the day on Friday then Nelson hadn't killed her. He didn't have any time.

Our next stop back at the Burke's house was a different story. James Burke, age sixteen, was home. So was his father, the Honorable Robert Burke. We met him in their living room. All of the windows were open in the room but it was stifling in there. The judge, a big man with a full head of black hair didn't seem very pleased to see us.

"What is this about?" he said firmly.

"I'm sure you are aware that there has been a murder in the neighborhood?" I said.

"Yes, I heard. Who wouldn't? Unbelievable in this neighborhood. I know Ham Gilford very well. I can't begin to understand the pain that he, and his family, must be feeling."

"It truly is sad," I said, "but we're not here to talk about the murder itself. We're here to talk about your son, James."

"James! You think my James had something to do with this heinous crime?" He was standing now and his face was becoming redder by the instant.

I put my hand up to calm him. "Not the murder, Your Honor. One of the neighbors told us that James will frequently walk behind some of the houses over there. They have seen him on numerous occasions back there, smoking cigarettes. We are just curious if he saw anything going on by the Gilford house at any time on Friday when we think the crime was committed."

I could see the judge calming down. "You don't suspect him of anything?"

"Not at this point, but I would really like to talk to him."

He nodded. "You have to understand that James is a bit addled. He gets confused easily and sometimes he will say things that make little or no sense. He's a sweet boy, wouldn't hurt a thing, but he just doesn't always understand what is going on around him."

"We'll be kind," I said. "May we speak with him?"

When I first saw James Burke, I didn't get the impression that there was anything wrong with him. He was a tall, young man with his father's dark hair and deep blue eyes. I could tell he was very shy and he didn't speak a word until spoken to. I let Keenan handle the questioning so I could observe.

"James," Keenan said softly, "we understand that you like to walk in the back of the houses along Illinois Street and smoke cigarettes."

"Yes," James said. His eyes were staring directly at the carpet he stood on.

"You know where the Gilford family lives?"

"Yes. Peter Gilford lives there."

Keenan looked over at Judge Burke. "Peter is in the same grade of school, but James doesn't attend the same school."

"Friday, four days ago, you were seen walking behind the houses over there, almost directly behind the Gilford's house. Did you see anything going on around the Gilford house? Did you hear or see anything? Did you see any people that maybe shouldn't have been there?"

James never raised his eyes to look at Keenan, but I could tell he had closed them. He was concentrating very hard and was silent.

"James is there something that you would like to tell these two detectives?" his father asked him.

James' eyes came open, but stayed down. He brushed some of his dark hair out of his eyes. "I saw the two angels by the Gilford house."

Judge Burke made some sort of audible groan. Keenan's face sagged. "What do you mean you saw the two angels by the Gilford house?" I asked

He nodded slowly and shuffled his feet from side to side. "The two angels were there. I was behind a tree. I saw them. They didn't see me."

"When you say two angels, you mean the type with white gowns and wings?" I asked.

"The two angels," James repeated slowly, eyes down.

Judge Burke stood and placed a hand on James' shoulder. "You can go now, son. Thank you for talking to the police."

James Burke turned and left the room. He never looked at us.

"I'm sorry," the judge said, "but that's the way it is most of the time. Sometimes we'll be talking, you know, just a normal conversation and he'll say something like the yellow flowers spoke to him that morning. It's very frustrating."

"I'm sorry," I said.

His lip trembled a bit and his eyes misted over. "It's tough. His mother left us when he was four. I get James the best care that I can find for him, but the doctor's tell me this is about the best that it's going to be for him. He is healthy, strong. He could live a long life, but for intelligence, he's not much smarter, and won't be, then he was when his mother left him.

•   •   •

"The two angels," I said out loud to Keenan in the carriage on the way to St. Regina.

"James Burke clearly had some issues that I can't comprehend," Keenan said.

"That whole interview was probably worthless."

"I guess there is a chance that he saw someone, but his description isn't very good."

"His description gives meaning to the word crazy."

"But no chance he had anything to do with the murder?"

"No chance. Consider the other two women. He's not involved. His whole world is sneaking around in the back of those houses, smoking his cigarettes and seeing angels."

"Maybe that's not so bad."

• • •

Sister Margaret Mary didn't look excited when we showed up again at St. Regina. She was out in the back of the school with a group of girls near a large wagon. Our friend Roger Duvall was there as well. He gave Keenan and I one look and then busied himself with preparing his horses for the trek they were about to make.

"I don't suppose you could wait until after I see this group of girls off?" Sister Margaret asked. There were maybe ten or twelve girls milling about the wagon. Most appeared to be around twelve or thirteen. They all wore a white blouse with a red sash across their chests.

"Are these the Daughters of the City?" I asked.

She smiled for once. "They are. Sister Helen will embark with them to the Forest Nursing Home. There they will visit with a group of elderly."

"We have a bit of an emergency," I stated.

Her smile disappeared. "Let me give Sister her last instructions."

She walked over to a short, plump nun who was joking with the group of girls. Seeing the sisters in their full habit reminded me again how hot it was. I had heard that they had been keeping records of Chicago temperatures and this year had been one of the hottest so far. As the pace of the day had been so fast, I hadn't noticed, but now I felt the heat and humidity. The back area of the school also smelled strongly of horse shit.

Sister Margaret Mary came back to us and beckoned that we follow her to her office. At least, we were out of the sun and a bit cool. "Now what is your emergency?" she asked.

"Another older woman named Agnes Gilford has been murdered. We think the crime occurred on Friday of last week. We were wondering if Mrs. Gilford is on any of your lists for being visited by the Daughters of the City."

Her face was expressionless as she dug into her desk for her ledger. She quickly flipped it open and turned over a number of pages. "I have never heard that name and from my records I can tell that we have never visited her."

I wasn't surprised, but I was disappointed. It didn't mean that someone who was connected to the Daughters couldn't be involved. Maybe it just meant that the killer wasn't exclusive to women the Daughters served.

"This seems like a terrible epidemic that you have on your hands, Detective," she said. "I guess it would be a lot better for everyone involved if you were able to solve it sooner than later."

I smiled at her. "My boss seems to think the same thing."

• • • •

In the carriage, on the way back to the precinct, I noticed Keenan scribbling furiously in his notebook. His head was down and he was engrossed in what he was writing. "Any clues in there for us?" I asked.

"No," he said. "Just trying to write down everything I can remember from our meetings today in case we need to recall them for a trial or a further investigation."

"Our word is not good enough in trial?"

"It's not our words that the prosecutors are questioning. It's our memory. Doesn't take much time and it helps to provide a better record."

I didn't push the topic. "We are going to need a vehicle."

"The police pool is still very small, but they have a few available."

"We need one."

"Is it for this case? We don't seem to be going very fast and don't see why we'd need to be in a hurry."

"We need the vehicle for surveillance."

He stopped his writing and closed his notebook. "But this is not some official investigation that we have been assigned?"

"Not official, yet."

"I don't know, Patrick. I am new to the precinct and I don't want to get in trouble doing something I shouldn't have been doing."

I considered this. "I am your superior, correct?"

"Yes."

"And if I tell you we are following leads you are supposed to assist me?"

"That is correct."

"All I want you to do is secure a vehicle and drive me around a bit. These are my orders. We haven't been assigned this case, but I think there is something going on. Our job is to investigate. That's what we're going to do. If we waited around for cases to be assigned to us we would miss half the shit that goes on in the Levee."

His look was skeptical. "I am just starting out my career. I don't want to get caught in the crosshairs. I also don't want to do anything to embarrass my uncle."

The great Bathhouse John Coughlin, I thought. "Keenan, you are a level one detective. I am a level three. You are simply following my orders. If something goes wrong I will take the blame and you can tell everyone that you were just doing what I told you. That would be the truth anyway. Make sense?"

He thought for a moment and looked out his side of the carriage. He finally turned back to me. "I understand," he said.

"Of course," I said, "with this little side investigation, you are not to tell anyone what we are up to."

His Adam's apple bobbed deeply. He nodded. "I understand that as well."

• • •

"I can see that someone who likes you very much has realized you were back in town," Stanley Kerjewski said. He was sitting in the Chicago Room on La Salle Street in the middle of the financial district. He had a big glass of red wine in front of him. He wasn't smiling.

"This?" I said. "This is nothing."

"Imagine my shock when I learned that you had returned to town. It probably matched my initial shock when I found out that you had left town. Of course, that was a good month after you actually had left town. Apparently I wasn't on the list of people you notified." Stanley and I had spent part of our early childhood together at Holy Trinity's orphanage. He had been adopted; I hadn't. He became a highly successful lawyer; I became a detective with a penchant for alcohol and opium.

"I left in a bit of a hurry. Things weren't exactly going my way."

"Shooting your immediate supervisor to death in an abandoned warehouse might give you that feeling."

"He was a murderer."

"So I've heard."

"You're not really mad, are you, Stanley?"

He smiled and sipped his wine. "Sit down, Patrick."

I took the seat across from him. He ordered me a glass of wine; I didn't object.

"So you went to New York and now you are back. You didn't like Manhattan Island?"

"I got involved in a nasty case there. It was resolved. Then word came that there was a nasty case here that they needed help with. I came back."

"Nasty cases in big cities. I don't suppose you get to deal with these types of crimes in places like Galena. What type of vile behavior brought you back to Chicago?"

My wine came and I took a sip. It sent a warm flash through my body. "Someone is having a rather splendid time of murdering old women. He ties them up in their own bedsheets and suffocates them with pillow stuffing."

I saw some of the sarcasm leave Stanley's eyes. I knew that his own adoptive mother was getting on in years. "I don't suppose you think that I might know a lawyer who likes to have fun killing older women?"

"I didn't come to see you for help regarding that case, but if you here one of your attorney friends bragging about the conquests I've described please let me know."

Stanley smiled. "I will, Patrick. What kind of information are you looking for?"

"Two pieces, really. First, I'm looking for some information on a former banker named William Winston."

"Former?"

"That is the correct word. He was with the First National Bank but disappeared in March. Left behind a very lovely wife, Lois, and a little boy, Freddie."

"What do you mean disappeared?"

"Just that. Here one minute, gone the next. His wife filed a report with the police, but they turned up nothing. The wife has moved on and assumes he's long gone."

"Who is your source?"

"The wife, Lois. She is my next door neighbor."

Stanley stopped a waitress and ordered another glass of red for him. "So you are trying to help this poor damsel find her missing husband?"

"Not that at all. He is definitely missing. I don't think he is coming back or will be found. I'd just like to find out about as much as I can about him up until he disappeared."

"That's sounds easy enough. I'll make a call over to the bank. I've got some solid connections over there."

"My second request might not be so easy."

Stanley's second drink came and he took a generous sip. His eyes were a little glassed and his cheeks had a glow. "What have you got?"

"A cop named Jack Garfield. A captain actually."

"Whoa. Stop there."

"What's wrong?"

"Are you talking about Black Jack Garfield? He works now out of the Central Station? He was one of the heroes of breaking the Haymarket case?"

"That sounds like the right guy."

"I don't know what Garfield has on you or what you think he is up to, but I know he is highly connected and very protected in the department. This is not a cop you want to mess around with and, anyway, there's probably not much I can find out about him that you don't already know."

Stanley's quick reaction surprised me. "But there might be something. Stanley, the bastard is starting an investigation of me because he thinks I killed my father and the husband of one of my key witnesses. I'm also pretty sure he sent some of his men to send me a message." I pointed to the bruises on my face.

He took a sip of his wine and rolled his neck to relive tension. "What do you think I can do?"

"Just ask a few questions. You deal with a lot of the higher ups in the department. As long as you don't sound like you're investigating Garfield, it might not sound suspicious. Maybe there's something you can find that will tell me why he has this vendetta for me."

"Did it ever occur to you, Patrick that you have an uncanny knack for getting under people's skin?"

I thought for a moment and smiled. "Not really."

Stanley rolled his eyes and took another swallow. "Let me see what I can find, but I'm not promising you much on Garfield."

I nodded. "Anything would be great, Stanley."

* * *

I would like to say that I behaved myself after that discussion, but that would not be the truth. After we finished talking business, Stanley and I each had a few more glasses of wine. I could tell that my old friend wasn't quite himself. As we poured the red wine into us his mood darkened. Something was bothering him, but I didn't press him and he didn't tell me anything. What I did notice was that he seemed in no rush to get home to his wife and children. He also didn't want to talk about Jack Garfield. When we finished one round of wine Stanley would order another. It was past eight o'clock when we finally got up to leave. Both of us were teetering just a bit.

The smart thing would have been to go right home, but I went to Coopers. Maybe it was Stanley's mood or maybe it was the death of the three older women. Maybe it had something to do with Jack

Garfield wanting to look in to my past. Whatever it was, it had put me into a bad mood as well. For some reason, I didn't think wine was what I needed. I resorted to bourbon. It was one of those nights where I drank in silence. I didn't want any company and none came seeking mine. I hardly remember any of the people that I saw. I don't remember how many drinks I had or what time I left the little tavern. What I do recall was how warm it still was when I got outside. That, and I also remembered that Christian Hanson had supposedly made an appearance at a tavern called Finn's over in Pilsen. That was where I instructed my carriage driver to take me.

Finn's was located on the corner of Halsted and Twenty-Sixth. It was a little place, but it was noisy as the carriage pulled up in front of it. I was aware enough to do two things before I got out of the cab. I told the driver to wait for me and I checked to make sure I was armed.

As soon as I entered Finn's the noise level lessened. I could tell the crowd of locals knew that an outsider had entered their realm. I was the only one dressed in a suit and tie. Most in the bar looked like wood shovers or longshoremen. I looked like a cop. When the entire place realized that I was standing there, the place became quiet.

I wavered a bit on my feet and for the first time I realized how drunk I was. I knew how dangerous Hanson could be and facing him in my current condition was ill advised.

"What can I help you with, fella," the bartender said. He was a big, burly type, wearing a white, stained apron. His bare arms looked about the size of a normal man's thighs.

"Hanson," I said, measuring the name carefully.

He cocked his head to the side. "Hanson? Don't know anyone named Hanson."

I took a deep breath. "Christian Hanson. Big, broad shouldered guy. Parts his blonde hair right down the middle. Also, he doesn't talk."

"Doesn't talk?" the bartender asked.

"Can't talk. He's a mute."

To my left there was a bit of noise, a chair being knocked over as two huge men, bigger than the barkeep, got up from their chairs and approached me. They got within ten feet when I drew my gun and leveled it at the head of the first man, the bigger of the two. "Far enough, assholes," I said. Both men stopped.

When I turned back to the bar, what I saw didn't surprise me, but I wasn't ready. The bartender was pointing a double barrel shotgun, fully cocked at my chest. I swallowed hard.

"Don't know this Hanson fella," he said. "Can't say that I know any mutes. What I can say is that I don't want any trouble in here, especially from the cops. I can also say that your best bet would be to turn around and walk out the door you came in because if I have to use this thing everyone in here will say how you drew your little revolver first."

There was a loud amount of grumbling and mumbling from the bar crowd. What I could make out told me that they were in agreement with the bartender.

"I just heard this man, Hanson, was in here last week and got himself into a bit of a knife fight."

The bartender shook his head. "I'm in here every night and I would know about something like that. Never happened and I told you that I don't know anyone named Hanson. I haven't seen him."

I didn't believe him, of course. I did believe his little sermon about blowing me to bits and then saying I'd drawn my gun first. With my history, there would be few that might not believe that story. The shotgun was still pointed chest high at me. I lowered my gun and put it back in the holster. The bartender did not lower the shotgun.

"When Hanson does show up tell him that Moses was here looking for him. That's all. He'll know why."

I turned and left Finn's. My coach was still waiting for me and I quickly climbed into it and told the driver to take me home. Even as the carriage started away from the bar there was no noise coming from within it. What I could hear was my heart. It was beating quickly and loudly. My temples tightened and my vision was mottled with bright, flashing lights. I yelled to the carriage driver to pull over and I was barely out of the cab before I threw up all over the street. I was, once again, a fucking mess. Thoughts of the basement opium den at Soon Lee's popped into my head, but for once my weak self prevailed. I climbed back into the coach and the driver made towards my apartment.

Other than dropping my keys onto the floor of my apartment building twice, I made it back to my apartment okay. I was drunk and couldn't believe that I had made it out of Finn's without a scratch or my head blown off. It had been a stupid move on my part.

When I finally got the key into my front door, I turned the lock and stepped into my apartment. I hadn't noticed the person behind me until I was well into my place and ready to plop into the living room chair.

"You don't look so good, Mr. Moses," the female voice said.

"Feel kind of shitty too," I said.

Before I could comprehend what was going on Lois Winston had turned on the lights and was helping me out of my suit coat and removing my tie. Then she undid my laces and pulled my shoes off. It didn't seem like much, but I felt a lot better.

"Back to your old fun and games, I see," she said.

I wasn't sure how Lois knew what my fun and games were, but indeed I had gotten back into them, at least one. "I just had a few drinks," I said, retelling one of the oldest lies in the book.

"More like a few dozen. You smell like a distillery." She left me for a moment and went into the kitchen. She came back with a cool rag and slowly wiped my face with it. I felt some life.

"That feels good," I said.

"You know, if you are not careful this kind of behavior will lead you back to where you were. That is self- destructive."

My mind and my eyes were clearer. Her dark hair was swept away from her face and I could see how beautiful she was, wearing some thin nightclothes. I could make out the outline of her body. I guess she saw me staring because she smiled. "Don't get any ideas," she said.

I was pretty sure I couldn't be much good at any kind of romance. What I wasn't so sure about was how Lois knew so much about my sordid past. I didn't have time to think about that.

"Some men were here looking for you this evening."

"Looking for me?"

"Well, they asked Freddie if Patrick Moses lived in this building and Freddie, smart boy that he is, came and got me."

"Who were they?"

"Well, they were driving a pretty big, new automobile. The driver was young. The guy that came out of the back seat when I came downstairs was a tough looking guy, broad shouldered, thick neck with a rough looking face. No doubt they were cops."

"What did they say?"

"The tough looking guy said he wanted to know if you were home. I told him no and asked if I could tell you who had called. He only smiled at me and said he'd be back. The two of them got back in the auto and drove off."

Jack Garfield, I thought, making house calls.

"Does this have anything to do with the guys that jumped you?" she asked.

"I'm sure it does."

"Well, based on you getting mugged and then having this guy show up here, maybe you shouldn't come in after dark and all liquored up."

"Maybe," I said. "Speaking of after dark, Lois, what are you still doing up? Don't you have to work in the morning?"

She smiled. "I do. It's just that my next door neighbor was making enough noise to wake the dead. I thought I'd better check on him to make sure he was alright."

"Thank you for checking, Lois, but I am alright."

She leaned down and kissed my forehead, like a peck a mother would give you. "I'm going to go now, Mr. Moses. Please try and get some rest. I'm sure you have a big day tomorrow. Also, watch out for that big, burly guy. I didn't like the looks of him."

Lois left my apartment, closing the door behind her. I was now very curious about why she knew so much about me. It was a little scary. What was scarier was what Jack Garfield wanted so badly that he came all the way to my apartment to ask me. As I tried to close my eyes, this thought was bothering me more and more.

*****

August 11th

Morning did come and with it came a nasty hangover. My head ached, my stomach lurched and my mouth tasted like I had eaten something dry and pungent. I got up to get a glass of water and that was more than an easy chore. I sat back down and drank the water. My body must have been so dehydrated because the water felt like blood was being infused back into my system. I had an instant jolt of energy.

More than anything in the world, I needed to eat. I had no food in the apartment which meant I would have to bathe and shave and get to a restaurant. Keenan was coming for me at nine. I wasn't sure I could wait that long. I also wasn't sure what time, if he was really coming back, that Jack Garfield might show. With great reluctance, I finished the water and got up to get ready. It was seven-twenty.

The shaving felt like it hurt, the blade scratching across my face. The bath felt much better. The warm water was rejuvenating me even though my temples ached, but they ached a lot. It was just past eight when I had finished cleaning up and had put on a clean suit. My hunger had abated a bit, but the wait for Keenan would still be tough. There was a loud pounding at my door.

I wasn't surprised when I opened the door to see Jack Garfield standing there. I had never seen him standing up, only sitting in his seat at South Side Park. As wide and thick as he was, he was also tall. His frame filled my entire doorway. Behind him was another younger man, smaller, but not by much.

"Good morning, Moses. Catch you getting ready for today?"

"You can say that. What do you want, Captain Garfield?"

"May we come in? It might not be pleasant to have this conversation out here in the hall."

I stepped aside and Garfield and his crony entered my apartment. Garfield walked to the window and turned. He took a few steps towards me. The other man stood to his side where he had a clear view of me.

"We stopped by earlier in the evening last night. I was hoping to get this interview out of the way then."

"I wasn't home. My neighbor, Mrs. Winston, told me you had come by."

"Yes. A lovely lady and with such a nice son."

"They are both very nice," I said.

"I came by here, but one of my associates had your trail most of the night."

"My trail? Were you following me, Captain?"

He smiled. "I was, Detective Moses. I always keep tabs on the people that I investigate because you never know where they will end up or what kind of mischief they may get into."

My stomach flinched. I didn't know if it was the hunger or the fact that Garfield had put a tail on me.

"I must say you had an interesting evening. First you had your little meeting with your attorney friend, Stanley Kerjewski. It went on a little long from what I understand. Rehashing old memories from the orphanage?"

I didn't care for his tone. "Something like that."

"Kerjewski is an interesting fellow. Came out of Holy Trinity like you did and has been extremely successful in the legal trade. Also has a lovely wife and children. Strange how the sins of the flesh can effect a man."

"What the hell are you talking about?" Stanley was one of the most loyal people I knew.

"It seems since you left Chicago that Mr. Kerjewski has found the pleasures of The Everleigh Club. There is a young girl that works there. Cora is her name. Mr. Kerjewski has grown quite fond of her. Of course, nothing in Chicago is a secret for long. There's always the threat that Mrs. Kerjewski might find out about this or even one of

Stanley's business foes."

"Is someone blackmailing Stanley?" I had wondered about his down mood.

Garfield shrugged. "I haven't heard that, but I guess it could be a strong possibility."

Again my stomach growled. "So why are you telling me this?"

"Just a bit of advice. Maybe if you cooperate with us, Mr. Kerjewski can get a proper warning to get out before he's in the shit so deep he doesn't know what to do."

"Cooperate with what?" I said loudly.

"First, I'm curious why you made that little late night stop at Finn's over in Pilsen. Not only did you go into a tavern when you were completely drunk, but you drew your service revolver as well. It's a good thing that bartender pulled out that shotgun or things could have gotten very ugly. What were you up to over there?"

"I was following up on a lead on an old case." It wasn't a lie.

"My men will go back there a little later today and speak with that bartender. We will find out exactly what you were looking for."

"I was looking for a bastard named Christian Hanson. He is a rapist and a murderer. Two of his murder victims were my past partners, Gunter Krause and Sam Walker. I got word that he had been in Finn's recently. I was following up."

Again the shitty smile. "Be careful next time. Your late night detective work almost got your head blown off."

"Well, I appreciate the warning about Stanley and for the advice about entering taverns in the late night hours. Now, I really must be getting my things together. I do have a busy day."

"Ah, yes. The Old Lady Murders as they are now being called. Three dead women and not one single clue from what I've heard."

What response could I make to that? It was true.

"I would like you to remember one thing before I leave you, Moses. Right before you left town for New York there were two very mysterious murders. Both involved people that you were connected to. One of them was your father, a good man. It is no secret anywhere in this city that the two of you did not get along very well. He was shot in the head on Christmas night.

"Next there is the death of Amos Stokes, not someone of major importance. We did ask around and find that Amos was a wife beater, not the best form of person. What is amazing was the fact that Amos' wife was a witness for you. She aided you in getting that nut Frank Pelicanos off the hook for saying he murdered your father. Seems she was seeing old Frank at the time your father was shot. Amos got word of this little dalliance and promptly beat the shit out of her. Few days later Amos gets shot in the throat while he was sleeping.

"Imagine that, two people that you were familiar with, getting plugged with a revolver of the same caliber that police officers carry in this city."

"There are a lot of police officers out there."

"But how many of them had ties to the victims like you did?"

"My father had many enemies, as you well know, and somebody, anybody, gave Amos Stokes what he deserved."

Garfield laughed loudly. "That's your defense."

"No defense. I don't need to defend anything."

He pointed one stubby finger at me. "I don't like you, Moses. I think you're a killer and I intend to find out. I want you to think hard about where you were when your father was murdered and when Amos Stokes was murdered. We are going to check around and see where you were those nights. You think real hard about your answers because they'd better match what we find."

Before I could respond any further, Garfield tore out of my apartment with his lackey trailing closely behind him. I walked to the window and watched as they got into their automobile and quickly drove off. My stomach grumbled again. This time I was pretty sure that it was hunger. Keenan wasn't due for ten more minutes.

• • •

After Garfield's auto drove off, I went downstairs and checked out the street. There didn't seem to be anyone lurking about. Maybe Garfield was bluffing about following me, but he had known where I'd been the night before. I wasn't willing to take a lot of chances. The day was overcast and didn't seem quite as hot as the past few. Any relief would be good. It was a little past nine when I saw an auto turn the corner and head in my direction. It got pretty close before I could see that it was Keenan behind the wheel. He smiled when he saw me. The brakes screeched loudly when he attempted to stop.

The car looked only marginally better than the one that Gunter and I had driven to Blue Island the past winter. By that, I mean that it had four tires and a windshield. The vehicle was dirty, dented and scratched in numerous spots. It had had a tough life. Keenan got out of the car and stood by it with the door open.

"What do you think?" he asked.

"It will do," I said quickly. "Now, here's what I want you to do. Drive south to Twenty-Ninth and then over to Logan. There's a diner there. I'll meet you there in five minutes."

"But I already ate."

"Then meet me outside and make sure nobody follows you there."

• • • •

When I had finished my breakfast, I climbed into the vehicle next to Keenan. Again, I looked up the street but so no signs of a tail.

"Where to?" Keenan asked.

"The precinct. Maybe we can figure out something from there."

The auto screeched again as Keenan turned her around and headed for the precinct. "I made sure that nobody was following me."

"They followed me last night, Garfield's men. They were on me from the time I met with my friend Stanley until I got home."

"No trouble?"

"Almost got my head blown off at Finn's when I went looking for Christian Hanson."

Keenan turned and looked at me. "Maybe you shouldn't make those trips without a backup. It's not safe."

"Watch the horse," I said pointing.

Keenan eyes came back to road just in time to miss a big plow horse. He swerved and almost ran into its' hindquarters.

"It's not that safe with you," I said.

He mumbled something and we continued the drive in near silence.

• • •

Sergeant Coogan was working the desk when we walked into the precinct. He was talking on the telephone when we entered the lobby and signaled to me with this hand. When I approached the desk he handed me a large, plain white envelope. There were no markings on it and I could see it had been tied shut by a little string clasp.

"What do you think it is?" Keenan asked.

"Don't know until we open it."

Instead of going up to my desk, I took the envelope downstairs to the crime lab. Harold Pinter was already there staring at something intently that was laid out on his desk. He looked up when I knocked on his door.

"Ah, Patrick, it's been an odd day already."

I was beginning to believe that every day in our line of work was odd. "Not too odd, I hope."

"The desk got a phone call. They transferred it to me because the caller said they had a clue."

"A clue to what?"

"Just a clue," Harold said. "I took the call and the person on the other end of the line sounded funny."

"What do you mean, 'funny'?"

"Just like I said. Their voice was muffled and high, not very deep."

"What did this voice say?"

Harold took off his glasses and wiped away a piece of lint. He grabbed a small piece of paper. "The voice said that Gavin McLeod hates his grandmother. That was the whole message and then the line went dead."

"Who is Gavin McLeod?"

"As I have heard you say many times, you are the detective."

I shook my head and placed the envelope on Harold's desk. "This was waiting for me when we walked in this morning."

Harold carefully undid the clasp and peered inside of the package. Then he tilted it to one side and two pieces of paper slid out. They landed on his desk right side up and we could see right away that they were sketches. Harold took a small tweezers and separated the pictures.

"Oh, my God!" Keenan said.

The pictures were drawn in pencil, all black. The first one depicted Agnes Gilford's cat hanging by the bedsheet from the lighting fixture in the living room. The drawing was done very well except that the poor cat's eyes were depicted at nearly popping out of his head. The second drawing was that of Agnes Gilford undoubtedly watching as her poor cat had been strung up. Agnes had not been blindfolded yet, but there were several bonds across her mouth and around her head. You could just see her eyes and the artist had done a magnificent job of displaying the pain that Agnes must have felt. The agony shown in her eyes was staggering.

"That poor woman," Harold said.

I nodded. "Not such a great day for the cat, either."

"God dammit!" Keenan said and turned and walked out of the room.

"Your young partner's not doing so well with death, is he?"

"That's not a good thing when we normally work with dead bodies."

I stuffed the pictures back into the envelope and left them with Harold. I followed Keenan upstairs. He had taken a seat on a bench across from the desk. Sergeant Coogan was off the telephone.

"You see who brought that envelope in for me, Coogan?"

"Sergeant Coogan, please Moses, and yes I did. Some old guttersnipe. Smelled like an old gin mill. Said it was for you and walked right out. I didn't think twice about it."

"How about the call you transferred to Pinter? The one where somebody said they had a clue?"

"That call? Thought it was very odd. I almost couldn't understand the person. Sounded like they were underwater or something. Said they had a clue on an important case. I thought they were nuts and since they didn't name the case I gave it to Pinter. He's the one around here working on all the clues."

"Okay. Thanks, Coogan."

His look told me he wasn't happy with me just using his last name, but he let it go this time. I walked over to where Keenan was sitting.

"Are you okay?" I asked.

He nodded. "Maybe I shouldn't work homicides."

"We'll worry about that later. What I need right now is for you to drive me into the financial district. I have a meeting there. While I'm in that meeting, I want you to check with the registrar's office in City Hall. See what you can find out about Gavin McLeod."

"The person mentioned in the phone call?"

"That's the one."

• • •

Stanley didn't look particularly happy that I had shown up at his office unannounced. At least, I had worn a suit and tie. The office was as top notch as you'd find in Chicago and lucky for me that it was only on the second floor. I walked up the flight of stairs happy that I didn't have to get on an elevator. The receptionist smiled politely at me until I told her I was a friend of Stanley's and didn't have an appointment. She said she would tell him I was here and to have a seat in the plush lobby. It wasn't long before she returned with Stanley right behind her.

"I told you it might take a little time before I could find anything, Patrick," he said once he had reached the lobby.

I looked at him and I could tell how beaten he felt. "We need to talk."

He didn't say anything further and led me back to his large office that overlooked LaSalle Street. He sat behind his desk; I took one of the chairs in front of it.

"I was going to call you," he said. "I called one of my old friends over at First National Bank and they were able to tell me quite a bit about William Winston."

I hadn't expected him to open with that topic. "Helpful information."

"It depends what you intend on using it for. William Winston was an up and comer with the bank. He was a graduate of the University of Chicago and a bit of a whiz with finance. He was rapidly moving up the ranks at the bank."

"Was?"

"Well, he disappeared. You already know that. What you didn't know was that Winston had started to make some very good money. Along with the money came a desire for loose women and a penchant for good scotch whiskey. According to my friend he was becoming a bit of a keg of dynamite. He started to show up for meetings late and half the time he was inebriated or well on his way. The bank was getting close to letting him go."

"But then he disappeared?"

"The bank was about a week away from giving him his walking papers when he just didn't show up for work. His wife came to the bank asking if anyone had any idea where he was. This was followed by the police with similar questions. After a while it was assumed that he was gone for good."

"Nothing missing from any of the accounts or files that he managed?"

"That was the first thing the bank worried about. Of course, they were concerned about Winston, but they checked their clients first. So far nothing has turned up missing."

"Was there any kind of life insurance on Winston?"

"Yes. The bank had him insured for ten thousand dollars. Again, there is no proof that he is dead so nothing has been paid out, but the bank believes the former Mrs. Winston is attempting to have a judge declare Winston dead. If she can get that documented then the bank's insurer would have to pay up. So far nothing on that front."

"Any idea where Winston did his drinking and whoring?"

"Sure, Patrick," Stanley said, smiling. "That would be The Evil Deed in the Levee. He was a fan of their scotch, their women and the roulette wheel. Maybe not in that order."

The Evil Deed was located on State Street and was one of many brothels owned by Big Jim Colosimo. I doubted that Big Jim had any idea who the clients were that ran through the place.

"There is one more thing I learned concerning Winston."

"Hopefully something that tells me where he is."

"I don't know about that. There was a little trouble at home. William and his wife attended a bank function for Halloween. Winston got very drunk and the couple went home. I guess he tried to push himself on his wife, but she was having none of it and gave him a black eye."

Sounds like Lois, I thought.

"He didn't care much for that so he punched her. The police were called, order was restored and no charges were filed."

I scratched at the back of my neck and felt one of my own bruises. "Only incidence of any violence?"

"Only one we know of," Stanley said. "So, that's what I was able to find on your Mr. Winston. So far nothing back on Jack Garfield. As I said to you last night, I'm not so sure I'm going to be able to find out much about him that you don't know."

"Is that because you can't or that you don't want to?"

Stanley sat back in his chair and stared blankly at me. A automobile horn sounded outside on La Salle. There was dead silence as Stanley looked at me. "Why would I not want to help you, Patrick?"

"What do you know about Jack Garfield?"

Stanley swallowed hard. "Well, you know this. He's a captain out of the Central Office."

"Not that stuff, Stanley," I said loudly. "Tell me why Garfield knows you would be seeing a young lady named Cora at the Everleigh Club. Also tell me why he finds it interesting that this little affair might cause damage at home or with some of your clients."

Stanley's face turned a bright shade of red. He rubbed his hand across it and through his hair. "Who told you about this?"

"Garfield."

"I started going to the Everleigh Club not too long ago," he said slowly. "I met this girl Cora, and I don't know how to explain this to you, but it was different and exciting. I was hooked, trapped. I started seeing her a couple of nights a week."

"Who approached you?"

"Not sure who they were, but they were two big guys. I knew they were cops. They grabbed me as I walked into the building about ten days ago. They said they knew all about Cora and me. They said they had enough to go to my wife or to some of my clients or competitors. I wasn't too concerned about the clients or competitors, but if they went to Karen, it would destroy her and probably ruin us. I'm sorry Patrick. I didn't mean for you to get dragged into this."

I waved my hand at him. "I'm just trying to keep you protected."

"How did Garfield know about this?"

"That's what bothers me. He seemed to know that this was going to happen, but he also said that if I cooperated with him on another investigation he could help you out."

"Well, I've learned my lesson. I haven't been back to Cora since they came and saw me. I guess I'm kind of waiting for the other shoe to drop."

"Just keep your nose clean for a bit, Stanley."

• • •

I hadn't been back to the Everleigh Club since my investigation of the death of Marshall Field Jr. back in December. I was greeted at the door by Ada Everleigh and she took Keenan and me into the main meeting room where her sister Minna was waiting for us. Both of the sisters were dressed for the evening, beautiful dresses and lavish jewelry, and it was only eleven o'clock in the morning. On this visit there was no offer of a beverage and neither sister looked very happy. Keenan, on the other hand, looked like a kid in the candy shop. His eyes were wide and alert as he looked around at the beauty of the club.

"You are not here to investigate another murder that supposedly took place on our premises, are you, Detective Moses?" Minna asked.

"No murder this time," I said. "I'm here for entirely different matter."

"And we see you have a different partner," Ada said. "Quite a young one."

"Keenan Coughlin, the Alderman's nephew," I said. Keenan was still dazzled by the beauty around him.

"Why are you here?" Minna persisted.

"I would like to talk to one of your girls. She may know something about a blackmail case. She may have seen one of the parties involved."

"Which girl would that be?"

"The only name I have is Cora. I would like to question her."

A sly smile came over Minna's face. "Ah, the lovely Cora James. One of our newest and most popular girls."

"She's the one I need to see."

The sisters looked at each other for a moment. I saw no change in expression or words exchanged.

"I will go get Cora," Ada said.

Ada and Minna both left the room, leaving Keenan and me alone in the grand space. "Quite a place," Keenan said. "Everything is so beautiful."

"The most beautiful thing about the whole place is the species that moves around on two legs."

Keenan smiled. "A lot of people think the Field kid was shot here."

"You hear a lot of silly things on the street," I said.

The door to the room opened and a woman walked in. She wasn't very tall and I could tell she had small features. She was wearing a robe and all I could see was her face which was a light brown color, deep brown eyes and dark hair. She closed the door behind her and turned to face us.

"Cora?" I said.

"Yes, sir." She looked frightened.

"Do you mind if I ask you a few questions?"

"Not at all, sir."

"Do you want to sit down?"

"I am fine standing," she said.

"We're here to ask you about one of your clients that you have been seeing recently. It appears that someone found out that he was seeing you and now they may try and blackmail him. This client's name is Stanley Kerjewski."

She bowed her head and closed her eyes. When she reopened them large tears rolled from them. "I never wanted to hurt Stanley."

I nodded. "Who are the men that approached you?"

"I don't know their names. They approached me when I left a business meeting and told me that they would tell Ada and Minna about me if I didn't help them."

"Don't give me a lot of bullshit, Cora. What kind of business deal were you leaving when these men approached you?"

She was busy wiping away tears. "An opium den. They were going to tell Ada and Minna that I was going there. It would cost me my position here. All they wanted was the name of some prominent people who came to visit me. If I gave them some names they wouldn't tell the sisters about me. I gave them Stanley. I am so sorry."

"You didn't give them anyone else?"

"Not yet. Just Stanley."

"And no idea who these men were?"

"No, but I'm supposed to see them at the Glitter Room tomorrow night at nine o'clock. They want more names. I don't have anyone else to give them."

"Don't worry, Cora. You go to the Glitter Room tomorrow. We'll be there watching. Nothing will happen to you."

She wiped away more tears. "Please tell Stanley I am sorry. He's such a nice man."

Dearborn Street was getting livelier as we stepped out into the midday heat and sun. The Levee District had a way of never quite going to sleep; the gambling parlors, bars and opium dens did business all day long.

"Where to?" Keenan asked. He had been extremely quiet during our talk with the Everleigh sisters and Cora. There was too much to see inside the building to get his attention away from it.

"There's a call box on that corner. Can you call your contact with the city and find out what they found out about this Gavin McLeod, the guy who hates his grandmother?"

Keenan looked down the street towards the corner. He looked a bit too long. "Is something wrong?" I asked.

"I'm not sure I've given them enough time to check him out."

"You won't know unless you call."

He didn't say anything further and turned to walk up to the corner. I leaned against the auto and looked up to the sky. The earlier clouds had cleared; the sun was beating down unhindered. It didn't seem that long ago that I was dealing with ice, slush and snow while looking for the Prostitute Murderer or trying to find the Hobbs' children. Then again, it seemed like long ago. Keenan was working his way back towards me.

"Any luck?" I said.

"He works for one of the trolley companies, a top executive. Believe it or not he lives right over by St. Regina, a little west of the parish, on Erie Street."

"St. Regina," I said.

"He just lives near there. Nobody said anything about him having anything to do with St. Regina," Keenan answered.

"Maybe just a bit of a coincidence."

"He's with Midwest Trolley. Probably a better chance that we can catch him at his office versus at home. Especially at this hour. I have that address as well."

"Let's go in that direction," I said, climbing back into the sunbaked vehicle.

• • •

The office for Midwest Trolley was located in the Loop on Adams Street. This was a lot closer than having to go all the way to McLeod's house on Erie. This was the good news. The bad news was that the office was located on the sixth floor. Keenan was walking ahead of me when the elevator came open on the first floor. There was no one else in it so he boarded it. By the time he turned around the door was closing and he was off to the sixth floor by himself. He was waiting for me there when I came out of the staircase.

"I'm sorry," I said, trying to catch my breath.

"You don't have to apologize," he said. "I had heard some stories about you having a fear of elevators. I thought they were crazy and didn't think about it when I got on."

"Oh, they're true. I don't know what it is, but the damn things defy logic. They seem to go up on their own. I just don't want them to come down quicker than they are supposed to."

Keenan wore a dubious look. "Are you okay to see Mr. McLeod?"

I took a deep breath. "I'm fine." I needed to get in better shape.

Gavin McLeod was the Chief Financial Officer for Midwest Trolley. He was a balding man, mid-forties, with a bulging belly underneath his suit vest. His face was young looking, but he looked concerned when we were seated in front of him.

"Can I ask what this is about?" he asked.

The office was very neat. McLeod's desk was covered with ledgers and accounting papers, all stacked very neatly. "You've seen something in the papers about the three older women who have been murdered in various parts of the city?"

His eyes went from mine to Keenan and back. "I saw something in the *Tribune* about it. Sounded like a horrible affair."

"It is very sad," I said, "and unfortunately we have very little in the way of leads. That's why we came by here to see you."

"Me!" he said. "What help could I possibly be in a murder investigation?"

"Our precinct is handling the investigation. We got a phone call this morning and the caller mentioned your name."

McLeod shot out of his chair much quicker than I thought a man of his girth could. He looked down on us. "What caller was this?"

"Please sit down, Mr. McLeod." He sat down quietly and looked embarrassed. "The caller seemed to disguise the normal sound of his voice. All he did was utter one sentence."

"What did he say?"

"He said that Gavin McLeod hates his grandmother."

"That's ridiculous," McLeod said. "My relationship with my grandmother has nothing to do with those murders. That caller has no idea what they are talking about."

"Why don't you tell me a little about your relationship with your grandmother?"

"There's not that much to tell."

"Then why would someone call our precinct and make that kind of comment. Someone must have some idea that this has something to do with our case. Either that or someone is trying to get you in trouble with us. Tell me about your grandmother."

McLeod sat back in his chair and laced his hands together in front of him. He was clearly thinking about the best way to phrase his answer. "I don't hate my grandmother," he said. "My mother died when I was four years old. My father had to work, of course, so my grandmother moved in to take care of me. I guess you could say she was devoted to me. She wanted everything to be just like my mother would have wanted it for me."

"That doesn't sound awful," I said.

"It wasn't by any stretch of the imagination. She did a lot of things for me that were beyond what even a mother would do for her child."

"So this comment about you hating your grandmother. Where would something like that come from?"

Tiny sweat beads appeared on his forehead; he didn't seem to notice. "As much as she did for me, she expected that I would give her the maximum effort in return. She was very tough on me. Chores, behavior, homework, grades, you name it. If I let up a bit in any of those areas I would hear about it. And she wasn't afraid to take the paddle to me. She was very strict."

Keenan cleared his throat and McLeod looked over at him. "Other than yourself," Keenan said, "who would be aware of the relationship that you had with your grandmother?"

"Well, my wife Alma for one. She thinks my grandmother was a tyrant." McLeod stopped for a moment and his face gained a worried look.

"You okay, Mr. McLeod?" I asked.

"Yes, I am fine. Something just occurred to me. Whenever our thirteen year old daughter, Lisa, misbehaves or falls behind in her studies we always tell her that she wouldn't have gotten away with it with my grandmother. She has asked us many times how tough she could be and we were truthful. She could be extremely tough. I suppose all of this talk could have given her an impression of my relationship with my grandmother."

"That you hated her and maybe because you hated her you wanted to take it out on some older women?" Keenan asked.

"That sounds preposterous," McLeod said. "I could see where Lisa might feel like I hated my grandmother, but I don't think it would go so far that she could interpret it to mean that I wanted revenge on old women."

"But she could have repeated what she felt about you hating her, if that was how she understood it?" I asked.

"She's thirteen," he said. "I suppose you can imagine that a thirteen year old girl will say just about anything."

"Where does she attend school? Maybe one of her classmates overheard her say something and called us to maybe try and help or maybe it was a prank."

"Well, she attends St. Regina, but they are out for summer break now."

Keenan and I looked at each other and stood quickly.

"Where is she now?" I asked.

"She's at home with her mother. Sometimes she goes out with the Daughters of the City, but not today."

• • •

The McLeod house was located west on Erie Street about a mile from St. Regina. It was a two story brick home and the front lawn and bushes were well maintained. Gavin McLeod accompanied us in our vehicle. He led the way into his home and immediately summoned his wife and daughter, Lisa. McLeod's wife was a thin, plain looking woman. She looked nervous because of the two police detectives that were standing in her living room. The daughter, Lisa, looked a little bit more like her father. She was a bigger girl with a little of her dad's girth. She looked more than nervous as she took a seat across from us.

"Lisa," I started, "I don't think there's much for you to be worried about. We're just here because of some comments that you may have made recently."

Lisa looked from me to her parents. She said nothing.

"Do you recall ever making any comments to any of your friends about how tough your dad's grandmother used to be on him?" I asked.

The poor girl looked to be on the verge of tears. Her mother handed her a handkerchief. "I didn't mean to," she said.

"That's okay," I said. "We're not here to get you in any trouble. We're just trying to track down who might have heard those comments and phoned our precinct about it."

Tears were rolling now and there were a few sobs. She got control of herself and took a deep breath. "We were all just talking one day about how are parents could always be so tough on us. All the girls had some sort of story where their parents had been really bad about something. I didn't really, but I told them how tough my father's grandmother had been to him. I told them she had often paddled my dad for misbehaving. I told them that as bad as my parents ever got, my father's grandmother could be a lot worse. She was some kind of a monster at times."

"Did you ever tell them that your father hated his grandmother?"

More tears flowed from her eyes and there were a couple of

muffled sobs. She wiped furiously at her face with the handkerchief. "I told them that I had the impression that things got so bad at times that my father ended up hating his grandmother."

The poor girl was really crying now and both McLeod parents were looking down at their hands. Someone had overheard Lisa McLeod make a rash comment and decided it was worthy of calling the precinct about it. That someone was likely a thirteen year old girl.

"Do you remember the girls that you told his to?" I said.

She nodded and I could tell that much further discussion was not going to take place. She was sobbing by now, shoulders shaking wildly. I asked her mother to take her into another room where Lisa could compile a list of the girl's names she had made the statement to. I assumed they were all members of the Daughters of the City. This meant another trip back to St. Regina for a visit with our friend Sister Margaret Mary.

• • •

We stopped by St. Regina on our way back to the precinct. Sister Margaret Mary was meeting in the Loop with the Archdiocese. She wouldn't be back until the late afternoon. We were told that the Daughters of the City were scheduled to meet at one o'clock the next day. That would be a good time to interview as many of the girls from Lisa McLeod's list as we could. We told the nun who helped us to let Sister Margaret know that we would be back tomorrow afternoon.

"So far," Keenan said, "we have a boy that saw angels and a teen girl spouting off about her father's strict grandmother."

"You see nothing promising there?"

He laughed a bit. "Those pictures that the killer sent to the precinct of Mrs. Gilford and her cat got me thinking a bit." We were driving south on Clark towards the precinct.

"Thinking about what?"

"Do you remember that at the second murder scene there was a book of drawings opened on the living room table? It looked like somebody had been leafing through it."

"We thought it might have been the victim."

"Right, but what if it was the killer? Whoever sent those drawings

134

to the precinct has artistic talent. Perhaps they have a strong interest in art. Maybe they were flipping through the sketch book at the murder scene." Keenan smiled.

"You're thinking that our murderer is an artist or someone who knows a lot about art?"

"From the drawings, a pretty talented artist. Is it so farfetched?"

I scratched my chin. The heat in the auto was unrelenting as we drove through the Loop. "Not at all, Keenan. In fact I'd say it's not bad at all."

Keenan smiled again. I even saw him blush.

• • •

I wish I could say that arriving back at the precinct was something that could help you maintain a smile or a good mood, but that would be a lie. Lieutenant Shipley wanted to see us as soon as we arrived.

"Update me on the murders, particularly Mrs. Gilford," he said. He was sitting behind his desk and looked worn out. "I understand there was a call with a lead and that someone dropped off some drawings of the murder scene."

"That is all true, but I don't know if I'd call the telephone call a lead."

"What do you mean? The person gave a name and said that person hated their grandmother."

"The person who mentioned that Gavin McLeod hated his grandmother was his thirteen year old daughter. She told it to members of the Daughters of the City. We're going to talk to that group tomorrow to see if we can find who made the call."

Shipley slumped in his chair. "What about the drawings?"

"Definitely the work of the murderer. Very well done, I'd say. Why he gave them to us other than to taunt us is a mystery."

"Nothing more than that, Moses?"

"At this time, no."

Shipley slapped his hand on his desk top. "Goddamn it!"

"Sir, I know when these cases get political that the pressure mounts. We've got a situation where there was very little to start with and not that much since. We're following anything we can."

135

Shipley nodded. "I know," he said. "I have the Chief and City Hall calling me regularly for updates. They are getting frustrated when I have so little to tell them."

"The moment we have something more definitive, you will be the first to know."

His eye roll told me I hadn't soothed his anxiety much, but he released us from his office. I went straight to my desk and called a friend at the payroll office in the Central Headquarters. Bobby Blake and I went through the Academy together. I ended up a detective. He got the shit beat out of him on the street and ended up on desk duty.

"Officer Blake," he said on the other end of the phone. Little or no excitement was shown.

"Bobby, it's Moses."

"Jesus. The return of the Legend. Haven't gotten yourself in any trouble yet?"

"Not yet. Look, I need a little favor."

"You didn't get it from me. People who associate too much with you end up dead."

I let the little sarcasm go. "I didn't get it from you. I need a home address on a cop named Daniel Bergman. He works on a task force with Captain Jack Garfield."

"I know him. He's a real bastard. You keep my name and yours out of any discussion about him, Patrick. Care to tell me what you need his address for?"

"He paid me a little home visit. I'm going to return the favor."

"Gimme ten minutes."

It took Bobby more like a half an hour to get back to me. Daniel Bergman lived on Division Street east of State. Not a bad neighborhood. Actually a real good one for someone on a detective's salary. On the way out of the door that evening, I told Keenan to get me at seven o'clock the next morning.

"Seven," he said. "That's a bit early."

"You know what they said about the bird catching the worm. We are going to track down something bigger and worse than that."

"Not going to tell me?"

"You will find out in the morning."

• • •

I paid a pretty penny at that time of day to get a carriage to take me west of the Loop. The last known residence for Lois Winston before her husband's disappearance, had been on Washington Street. The house was a nice looking, one story bungalow with a perfect lawn and colorful flowers blossoming in pots surrounding the front porch. It wasn't the current residents of Lois' old home that I cared to talk with. It was her neighbors.

I knocked on the neighbor's door to the east and the door was opened by a younger woman, a little dodgy looking, with a toddler hanging onto her dress. The woman looked a little bit under duress and didn't look like she'd be particularly cooperative. I smiled and showed her my badge. She smiled in return.

"What can I do for you, Officer?"

"My name is Detective Moses," I said. "I am hear following up on the investigation into William Winston's disappearance. Do you have a minute?"

The toddler, a thumb sucking boy of around two, made some sort of cranky noise and his mother knelt down and whispered something into his ear. The little boy smiled and was quiet. "Sorry," she said. "Come on in. The house isn't very clean."

I entered the house and quickly found out that she wasn't lying. The area of the house I could see seemed like one big collection of clutter. There were clothes and toys and papers laying all over the place. The place also had a musty smell.

"I didn't know Mr. Winston very well," she said. "I would see him once in a while and he would say hello, but that was about it."

"How about Mrs. Winston?"

"Lois? Lois was very nice and so was her boy, Freddie. He would play with Arnie whenever we were outside. It was sad when they moved away. Of course, this was after Mr. Winston left."

"You think he left? We were under the impression that this was a disappearance."

"What's the difference?"

As I looked closer I could see that the dress she wore had many stains on it. Her hair didn't look like it had been washed recently.

"Well, in a disappearance there is the possibility that something bad happened to him. When you say he just left that gives us the idea that he had some motivation for leaving his family and a great job behind. Do you see what I'm saying?"

She seemed to be thinking on it. "Maybe saying that he left isn't accurate."

"You have no solid reason for thinking he would have a reason to leave?"

"No. Like I said, I would only see Mr. Winston once in a while. Most of what we said was hello and goodbye. There wasn't much formal conversation. Really, the more that I think about it, he was here one day and then gone the next. It seemed to really bother Lois and little Freddie, but that's expected."

"The Winston's were good neighbors?"

"There was nothing bad about them. I do miss her gardening. The front of their house still looks pretty good with the new owners, the Fawcetts, but they've let the back go a bit. Lois was always very particular about her garden. Worked at it all the time. She always had a nice flower garden in the back and she built that lovely berm. That was her pride and joy, that berm."

Lois Winston's neighbor on the west was a middle aged woman named Phyllis Martin. Unlike the first neighbor, Phyllis Martin, wore a clean dress and her living room was spotless. I also saw no signs of any messy toddlers.

"Lois was the sweetest girl," she said, "and little Freddie was an angel. I couldn't have asked for a nicer neighbor."

Phyllis Martin's hair was just starting to go gray. She had rosy cheeks and not many wrinkles on her face.

"What about Mr. Winston?"

Her expression changed. "I didn't know William very well. He would say hello and things like that, but that was about it."

"What do you think happened to him?"

She suddenly stood and walked to her front window and looked out across her lawn as if she was expecting someone. She turned to face me. "I think he ran off with one of those girls he was seeing on the side. Can you imagine a man acting that way, seeing other women while you had a wife and child at home?"

I thought of Stanley and other men who I knew who had fallen victim to sins of the flesh. I didn't feel like I was in a good spot to comment. "What makes you think he ran off with a girl? He left a great job behind here in Chicago."

She looked back out the window. "I thought I'd hear from Lois by now, but it's been nearly five months. I guess she's settled down and gotten on with her life."

"She's doing fine, Mrs. Martin. Back to the question. Why do you think William Winston would run away with a girl?"

"It's been so long and I don't think anything will come out of it anyway."

"What are you talking about?"

She faced the window as she spoke. "William wasn't always very nice to Lois. He would call her names and say terrible things to her. Most of the time this would happen when he was drunk. He would tell her that the girls downtown were a lot nicer to him than Lois was. They could give him what he wanted. As he became a bigger drunk the stories got worse. He would call Lois a whore and other names."

"Where was Freddie when all of this was going on?"

"It would depend. Sometimes it was late at night and he was asleep. Sometimes it wasn't that late and Freddie would hear a lot of it."

My stomach tightened. "Did he ever hit Lois?"

She looked at me with a thin smile. "Detective Moses, what do you think?

I nodded. "Did William ever threaten Lois that he might leave her?"

"All the time. When he got that drunk mouth going he would tell how he could have such a great time, and have more fun, if he lived near the Loop. He told her he was bogged down with a wife and a kid. He had made a mistake marrying her."

"Do you think Lois thinks he just left her?"

"Not at all. She's convinced, and swears by it, that William got in trouble down in that Godforsaken Levee District. He was losing a lot of money playing roulette. Lois is convinced that he ran aground with the wrong people and he was murdered and his body was dumped somewhere. Of course, without a body, they can't legally declare him dead."

"Which means she can't get the life insurance?"

"Correct. At some point, if there's no sign of William, he will be declared dead and she'll get her money."

• • •

I was tired and not that hungry when I got back to my apartment. All I wanted was rest and to be alone. I hoped to avoid any contact with Lois Winston. This might not be that easy. Freddie was on the front porch. He seemed to be in a bit of a trance as I walked up to our building; his eyes were looking straight across the street.

"You doing okay, Freddie?"

This snapped him out of his little daze. "Hello, Mr. Moses. I'm doing fine."

Even his cadence sounded a little off. "What are you doing sitting out here all by yourself?"

"Mom has a visitor over. She asked me to wait out here until she came out to get me."

"I see. You want some company?"

He shrugged. "Sure."

I sat down on the steps and removed my hat. It was almost seven and the late summer sun was setting, but the air was still tinged with heat and humidity. "Anything special happen today?"

"Nope. Nothing special, but some men came by a little while ago, right about the time that I came out here. They wanted to know if you were around. They asked me if you were upstairs."

I ground my teeth together, thinking of Garfield and his thugs. "What did you say to them?"

"I told them that you weren't home and I didn't know when you would be."

"Did you happen to notice if one of the men was limping real bad?"

He thought for a moment. "Nope. Nothing like that. This one guy was real scary looking. A big guy with yellow like hair. He didn't say anything. The other two men did all the talking."

A big guy with yellow like hair. "This big guy with yellow like hair, how did he part it? Was it to the side just like mine?"

Freddie looked at me as I pointed to my part with my finger. "No. He had a very clear line right in the middle of his hair."

Now Christian Hanson was visiting me, I thought. "Freddie, the next time you see those men, I want you to go inside and call my precinct and have them find me. Do you understand?"

He looked frightened. "Are they bad men?"

"They are very bad men, especially the one with the yellow hair. If you see them again, run inside."

He nodded and looked up and down the street. "The one with the part in the middle, when they were ready to leave he walked up to me and pointed a finger at me like a gun and then he walked away."

"Everything will be fine. Just listen to what I say."

At that moment the door to the building opened and a tall, thin guy in a suit came out. He was still doing his tie when he stepped onto the porch. He looked drunk and had lipstick on his cheek. "Frankie, your mom said to tell you it was okay to come upstairs."

"It's Freddie," I said.

He stopped for a moment and straightened up. "Who the fuck are you?" he said.

I smiled. "I'm Detective Patrick Moses. I'm Freddie and Lois' next door neighbor. And you are?"

"Robert Cotton. Doctor Robert Cotton."

"No shit," I said. "Is there a Mrs. Cotton."

He got a puzzled look. "Hey, Detective, I'm not trying to get anybody into any trouble or anything. Lois and me, we're just good friends."

"Uh huh. Well clean the lipstick off your face before you get home or the real trouble might begin."

"Oh shit!" Robert Cotton said as he stumbled past us. He walked to a newer looking automobile without looking back at us. Soon he was driving away.

"I didn't like him either," Freddie said.

I ruffled his hair. "You're a smart boy."

• • •

Later there was a knock at my door. I had finished eating and was quietly reading the paper. I wondered for a minute, got smart, and grabbed my revolver. "Who is it?"

"It's Lois, Mr. Moses."

I opened the door and there was Lois standing there in her nightclothes again. She looked completely refreshed and smelled good, too.

"May I come in for a second?"

I slipped my gun into its holster and let her in. She really was pretty.

"I'm sorry for the position that I put you in earlier this evening. I had company and I know it's probably not right, but I told Freddie to wait outside for a bit."

"None of my business, but do you think it's right to bring a married man home to your apartment?"

She blushed. "How'd you know he was married?"

"It wasn't even eight o'clock and he was in a big hurry to get out of here."

"You're right," she said. "I just get so lonely sometimes. I'm sorry for what I did to you and Freddie. It wasn't right."

"Forget it. It's just that Freddie looked a little worried when I saw him on the porch. I thought something was really bothering him."

"I just don't think he's gotten over his dad leaving us the way he did. It wasn't that long ago. I'm sure seeing me with another man didn't make him feel very good."

"I'll talk to him. I knew my father, but hated him. I've never seen my mother and it bothers me."

"That would be nice."

"Lois, you just said your husband left you guys. Before you said he disappeared, like maybe something happened to him."

"That's what I meant," she said quickly. "I think something bad happened to him, but no one seems to know."

Lois left soon after that. I was left wondering whether William Winston had left them or whether something bad had happened to him and someone made him disappear. We had a big day tomorrow so I wanted to turn in. Keenan didn't know it yet, but we were going on an early surveillance of Daniel Bergman, the Garfield henchmen I had stabbed in the leg. After that it was Sister Margaret and the Daughters of the City. Last we had our meeting with Cora at The Glitter Room. My temples tightened as I thought of all the loose missing pieces that were out there. I hoped soon that some of them would fit together. Before I turned out the lights and went to bed I made sure both doors were securely locked. I also placed my gun on the table right next to my bed. Christian Hanson visiting your house was not a welcome thing.

*****

August 12th

Surprisingly, I slept well. I was awake, cleaned up and had something to eat well before Keenan showed up. I looked outside of my front window and could see that it was a good day to keep an eye on someone. There was a light rain falling and the sky was filled with dark, heavy clouds. At least, for the time being, it looked like we would be stuck in the gloom. It also meant that the heat and humidity would be gone, until the sun reappeared.

I saw Keenan pull up in front of my building at exactly seven o'clock. I left my apartment, stopping briefly by the Winston unit, but there wasn't any noise coming from there. When I got in the car Keenan was wearing a big smile.

"Is it your birthday or something?" I asked.

"No. Just in a good mood. Where are we off to so early?"

I gave Keenan the Division Street address that Bobby Blake had given me. His face registered nothing different. "What's there?" he asked.

"A little surveillance," I said. Keenan put the auto into drive and we were off.

The building that Daniel Bergman lived in was a two story, brownstone a little east of State Street. I knew this area well. There were a lot of affluent people living around here. Bergman was a Chicago Police Department Detective. I knew their pay scale. Unless he married wealthy, there was no way he could afford this neighborhood on his salary. We were parked about a half a block down with a clear view of the stairs and door leading to his building.

"Who are we watching?" Keenan asked. His earlier smiling mood had changed a bit.

"You'll see in one moment."

We waited quietly for a good half hour. The rain was coming down harder and we had the windows rolled up. It was starting to get warm in the car.

"We should probably check in with the precinct and tell them what we are up to," he said.

At that moment a big vehicle drove past us and stopped directly in front of Bergman's building. The door to the building opened and a big man walked out, taking the stairs cautiously. It was clear he was limping badly. He walked up to the auto and got ready to get in. "That's our boy. Not too close, but don't lose him."

"Who is he?"

"His name is Daniel Bergman. He is a detective that works for Jack Garfield."

"A police detective?" Keenan asked. "What has he done that we are about to follow him?"

"That's what we are going to find out."

The vehicle up ahead of us pulled out and Keenan followed as closely behind without being noticed. It was raining so hard right now I wondered if they could see twenty feet behind them. The car didn't go far. It stopped in front of a tavern on Clark Street and Bergman got out, limping badly, and entered the place. He wasn't gone long, maybe ten minutes, before he was back and the car was moving again. This time they turned east and picked up State. They turned there and in another minute Bergman was out of the car and into a new bar.

That morning he made seven stops before the car go onto Chicago Avenue and was heading for Police Headquarters. The whole time we were watching Keenan would ask what was going on. I told him to be quiet and I'd tell him later. When Bergman's car pulled into the parking area for headquarters, Keenan pulled over and turned the car off.

"You need to tell me what is going on," he said. "I have been driving through the rain and the mud for the last hour and a half following a cop. I'd really like to know what we are up to. I have a right to know."

"You're right," I said. "You do have a right to know."

We were silent for a bit. "Are you going to tell me, Patrick?"

"I think Bergman and some of the cops that work with him, including his boss, Jack Garfield, are into extortion and blackmail. I think what we watched today was Daniel Bergman fleecing bar owners. I'm sure they are telling these owners that they will be protected as long as they make their regular payments. It wouldn't surprise me if these cops are the same ones bothering Roger Duvall, forcing him to steal from Bower's Meats. I'm pretty sure they are behind a blackmail scheme involving my good friend, Stanley Kerjewski, and that girl Cora at the Everleigh Club."

Keenan swallowed hard. "What are we going to do?"

"Sit tight for a bit. All of this is conjecture on my part. I don't have any real proof. I do know one thing. When you go after cops you'd better have solid proof."

"Can't we just go back and ask those tavern owners why Bergman stopped in there in this morning?"

"Yes, we could, but I doubt they'd tell us anything. They are probably okay paying a little fee to be left alone. If word got out that they ratted on these guys it could be a lot worse for them than paying a few dollars a week."

I could see Keenan thinking hard. "This is not a case we have been assigned."

"We haven't been assigned this case because nobody but us knows about it."

Keenan didn't respond. He restarted the car and got us headed back towards the Levee.

• • •

The group of girls looked restless, but not overly concerned that the police wanted to talk with them. We had met with Sister Margaret privately and had repeated the whole story of what had happened between Lisa McLeod and her father. The good Sister was alarmed that one of her girls might have made a prank call to the precinct and she had agreed that we could talk with them. She had them all gathered in one of the classrooms. When we walked into the room all of the chatter that had been going on ceased.

"This is Detective Moses and this is Detective Coughlin. They have come here to talk to you girls about one of the cases they are working on," Sister Margaret said. The girls listened attentively. "If you have any knowledge of anything that they are talking about, please tell them. This is a very serious matter."

Most of the girls had their eyes glued to us; a few shuffled their feet. One girl in the back of the group raised her hand.

"Yes?" I said.

"Does this have anything to do with those old ladies that have been murdered? My father told me about them."

"Let the detectives ask the questions," Sister Margaret said.

The young lady that had asked the question blushed and lowered her eyes.

"One of your classmates," I started, "Lisa McLeod, made a comment to the group of you. She said something like her father Gavin McLeod hated his grandmother. Do any of you recall Lisa making this kind of comment?"

Again there was some foot shuffling and not too many of the eyes were looking at us.

"You won't get in any trouble if you just recall her making the comment and either will Lisa. She said that she had done so," I said.

After a few moments five hands out of the eleven raised their hands. The rest looked at them as if they knew they were in trouble.

"The six of you that didn't raise your hands may leave the room," I said.

The small group of six left the room, closing the door behind them.

"So you all heard Lisa make the comment?"

There were five yesses, some not very loud, but the group all agreed.

"There was a phone call made to our precinct the other day. The caller just said that Gavin McLeod hated his grandmother. The caller made sure to disguise their voice. What I am trying to determine is if any of you made the call to the precinct or if you told anyone outside of the Daughters of the City about what Lisa said."

The girls all looked at me wide eyed. There wasn't a sound amongst them.

"If any of you made that call, I would recommend that you come forth now and admit it," Sister Margaret said. "This may be important information for the police. I will promise you that you will not get into any trouble if you admit to making the call."

More foot shuffling and no more noise. All five girls were saying nothing.

"None of you knows who phoned the precinct?" Sister Margaret asked.

Nothing.

"And not one of you five recalls telling anyone outside of our group anything about what Lisa McLeod said?"

Nothing.

"I think we are done here," I said. I looked at the girls. "If any of you knows anything about the answers to either question you can call me at the precinct and tell me privately. All we want is information, particularly if someone else outside of your group knows what Lisa said. No one will get in trouble."

Again the small group was silent. "You may all go," I said.

Four of the five girls left the room. There was one girl left, the one who had asked the question about the case that we were working on.

"Do you have something to say to the detectives, Patricia?" Sister Margaret said.

Patricia was one of the taller girls in the group. She was at that awkward state that a lot of teenagers go through. "I was just curious why someone would kill a bunch of old women like that. They seem kind of helpless to me. It just seems totally cruel."

"That's probably the main reason," I said. "There is, unfortunately, a lot of cruelty in the world. There can be no other explanation for it."

She nodded and I noticed how sad she looked. "You will catch him, won't you?" she asked.

I smiled to make her feel better. "We will catch him."

"My grandmother is eighty-seven. I'd feel awful if someone hurt her," Patricia said. There were tears rimming her eyes.

"I don't think you need to worry. The killer has acted rather randomly. I don't think you need to worry about your grandmother."

A couple of tears slid down her cheeks and she wiped them away. She nodded. "Okay," she said.

"Run along now, Patricia," Sister Margaret said.

The girl left the room. "She's a very emotional young girl. I appreciate you taking the time to talk with her."

"It's no problem, Sister, but now we have taken up enough of your time. Please let us know if you hear anything more on your end."

"I will, Detective Moses, but please do one favor for me."

"What would that be, Sister?"

"Please catch this bastard."

• • •

"Do you think one of those girls made the call to the precinct? Keenan asked.

"A lot of them heard Lisa McLeod make that comment about her father. Either one of them made the call or they told somebody what she said and they made the call."

"I see that," he snapped, "but we're not anywhere closer to finding out who is killing these women."

His tone of voice showed a lack of patience, but I said nothing about it. "These cases are like puzzles. Little pieces fit and sometimes they are the biggest reason you can put some of these things together."

"Shipley is going to lambast us for not coming up with something a little better than that."

"He might, but that is a tremendous problem within the department. We have a lot of authoritative types who have spent little or no time on the street. Just because someone upstairs calls them and says that so and so is upset because it's taking time to solve a crime doesn't mean anything. They get solved when we have clues or evidence that leads us to the killer. Right now we have very little so it is a good idea to collect pieces. Understand?"

"And the pieces we were collecting on Daniel Bergman this morning?"

"Just more pieces, but to a different puzzle. We are just getting started on that puzzle."

"But it could mean nothing."

"Maybe, but I doubt it."

We drove the remainder of the way to the precinct in a driving rain and total silence. When we parked the car and walked into the building we almost got soaked.

"Shipley was looking for you," George Loftus said.

"I assumed that," I said. "City Hall is pestering him to solve these murders because of the Gilford lady. I wish it were that simple."

"Who is killing these women, Moses?" Loftus asked.

"Somebody who is doing it just for fun."

"It does seem like you draw all of the cases with the truly sick individuals."

I hadn't thought of it that way, but I'd had my share the last year.

• • •

"We'll meet here at seven-thirty," I told Keenan. "I want to get to The Glitter Room in time to set up for Cora's visit with these cops that are using her."

"That sounds fine. Dinner plans?"

"I'm meeting an old friend, but I'll be back in time."

"Going anywhere special?"

I shook my head. "We haven't decided yet."

It was past five when I slipped down the hall to use the lavatory. There is a rear exit back there that is seldom used. I used it that night. I slipped down the stairs and called for one of the carriages that linger outside of the building. It was still gloomy looking and there was a light drizzle falling. As we pulled away, I looked back. No one had followed me out of the exit.

My dinner plans were to meet up again with Roger Duvall, the wagon driver for the Daughters of the City. He had spent time in prison for a sex related charge and some cops were using this information to get him to steal beef for them. I had an idea what ring of cops were behind this.

Duvall wasn't home when I pounded on his door. Luckily there was a massive oak tree in front of his building. Amazingly, this tree provided nearly dry conditions under it. I leaned against the tree and waited and hoped that Duvall would come along shortly. I didn't have that much time.

After about fifteen minutes, I saw Duvall approaching the building. It had finally stopped raining so he wasn't in any particular hurry. I was.

"Good evening, Roger," I said from underneath the oak.

He looked at me and squinted. "Oh shit!" he said.

"Can I have a minute of your time?"

He spread his arms. "What choice do I have, Detective Moses?"

I smiled. "Let's go inside."

Duvall's apartment didn't look any better than it had the first time. From all the moisture in the air it smelled mustier.

"What do you want?"

"The cops that are bracing you for the stolen beef. Still having a problem with them?"

"They haven't gone away," he said quickly. "If I don't give them what they want they go to the owners of Bower's Meats and the priests at St. Regina and tell them the truth about my background. There goes my jobs."

"So you grab the extra beef from the warehouse and then they meet you and you transfer it to them?"

"That's how it works."

"When is your next meeting?"

He eyed me warily. "Why?"

"Roger, you are about to be liberated from your burden."

Now he looked real worried. "You can't fuck this up for me, Moses. These guys are serious types. They can cause me all types of problems."

"Don't worry about that. When is the next meeting?"

"It's tomorrow at ten o'clock at Farrell's Market on Erie and Wabash. I promised them a crate of steaks."

"Ten o'clock?"

"That's when I told them I thought I could get to the market."

"Try to act a little surprised when we show up."

"When who shows up?"

"The cavalry," I said.

"These guys are a little crazy and they are armed."

"The nice thing about being with the police is that they give you a gun, too."

The look on his face showed that I had not instilled much faith in him with my comment.

• • •

I stopped at Cooper's for one drink before heading over to the precinct to meet Keenan. One neat whiskey was what I needed to help clear my head. By coincidence or luck I had stumbled onto an extortion ring managed by my new friend, Captain Jack Garfield. As I told Keenan, cases get solved by eventually placing pieces into the puzzle. I knew Garfield had set up Stanley with the prostitute, Cora.

I was also pretty sure they were picking on Roger Duvall, threatening his livelihood if he didn't cooperate with them. I'd also seen them fleecing tavern owners that morning. Tomorrow would tell me a lot when Duvall met his contacts. I didn't know if they were Garfield's men, but the fit seemed right. Of course, if the same crew showed up tonight at the Glitter Room, we might not need to see Duvall tomorrow, but I had my reservations about this meeting.

The Lois Winston matter continued to intrigue me. Had her husband disappeared through violence as she maintained or had he just left town. Usually dead bodies show up and, so far, there was no body. Why would Winston leave a great job? For another woman? That seemed unlikely to me. You could leave your wife and kid, but would you leave town? I shook my head and ordered a second whiskey. The first one hadn't quite cleared my head.

The three dead older women kept gnawing at me. Three separate, but related murders and we had very little to go on. Why had the killer sent us pictures? Did he want us to catch him? Even then, two pencil sketches didn't tell us much about him. I thought that he was just trying to play games with us.

As I twirled the last bit of bourbon in my glass and got ready to go meet Keenan, I thought of my last little problem. I had gone seeking Christian Hanson in a drunken state. He had returned the favor and came looking for me. For someone who had always been so secretive about his whereabouts this was a different move. Maybe he was tiring of the cat and mouse game and came to my apartment seeking the end to it. That thought made me shudder a bit. The man was crazy.

• • •

The Glitter Room was one of those places that doubled as a gambling house and a brothel. Whatever you went there for you were likely to leave with less money than you came with. That's what kept the place thriving and the owners happy. Unfortunately, at least for Keenan, it was not nearly up to the standards of the Everleigh Club. There were no ornate chandeliers or golden piano, but it was relatively clean. It was several notches up from Bed Bug Row, but that didn't mean one of the girls wouldn't stab you if you tried to cheat them.

Luckily for us, I knew the Madam, a stern looking matron named Carol Marker. I told her exactly what we were there for, a sting. She told me that was fine as long as there was no shooting. She also said that if we broke anything we would have to pay for it. I agreed to those terms and told her that Cora would just hang out in the front near the faro tables. Keenan and I sat across the room. I saw no harm in ordering another whiskey. Keenan didn't want a drink.

"You nervous?" I asked.

"Yeah. A little. I don't like all of this sneaking around on cops."

I took a sip of the whiskey and watched as Cora told a potential customer she wasn't working and the man moved on. "These are crooked cops as far as I can tell," I said. "Remember, it is our job to stop crime, even if the case has not been officially given to us."

"There won't be any shooting, will there?" He was obviously well aware of my recent history.

"Let me put it to you this way. I don't plan on there being any shooting, but if they draw their guns and intend on using them on us, then I recommend shooting back. Also there is no code that says that they have to shoot first. Following that rule will get you killed very fast. "

I saw two guys enter the gaming room. One was very tall and thin; the other looked like a fat, little ball. They didn't seem to fit the description of any of the guys that jumped me and they weren't Daniel Bergman. They walked around the room a bit, sizing up their odds, and showed no interest in Cora. Finally, they took two seats at a faro table and placed some money in front of them for the dealer.

"Just gamblers," I said.

It got to be ten past nine and I could tell that Cora was getting agitated. She kept moving, changing her sitting position on the couch. Frequently she would check the door when someone walked into the room. She was constantly biting at her lower lip. Finally, she lit a cigarette and closed her eyes for a bit.

"She's getting impatient," I said.

"Maybe they won't come," Keenan said.

"They are looking for a new mark, someone they can force into a corner and make some money on. They will come."

As it got close to nine-thirty, I saw that Keenan was right. They weren't going to come. I wasn't sure our little scheme would have come off cleanly anyway. Cora was fidgeting like crazy, biting her lip and twisting her hair in her fingers. I doubted she could carry off a sensible conversation with anyone. On top of that, Keenan was very nervous as well. He was sweating profusely and I could hear him taking deep breaths to relax his nerves.

"Time to go," I said.

He exhaled loudly, like he found out his favorite aunt wasn't going to die. I walked across the room and Cora almost jumped out of her shoes when I mentioned her name.

"You sure they said the Glitter Room at nine o'clock?" I asked.

"That is what they said, Detective Moses," she said, still playing with her hair and nibbling on her lip.

"Well, they are not coming. It's time to get out of here."

The look of relief on her face was palpable. Between her and Keenan, I couldn't tell who was more nervous.

"Am I free to go?" she asked.

"Yes, but I want you to let me know if you hear anything more from these guys. Understand?"

She nodded and was out of the place quickly. I felt my temples tighten and thought of Soon Lee's. I closed my eyes for a second and the pain and the urge went away. Keenan was still standing there. He looked alive again.

"Do you need me for anything, Patrick?"

I thought of the potential meeting with the cops who were hustling Roger Duvall. I wanted to keep that quiet. After watching Keenan tonight I knew he wasn't up for it, anyway. "I think we're good."

"Should I pick you up in the morning?"

"There's nothing urgent that I can think of. I'll just meet you at the precinct."

He gave me a bit of a puzzled look. "Okay," he said and he turned and left the place.

I could stay here for a bit and have a drink or two and maybe get myself in trouble with a lady, but my brain told me to take the easier route. I walked out of the Glitter Room and headed in the direction of Cooper's.

*****

August 13th

I wasn't sure that the shining sun that came up the following day was a good omen. I didn't believe in that stuff anyway. What I knew was that I had a nasty hangover with a decent headache. I managed to get out of bed and get ready and over to the precinct before eight o'clock. Keenan had not yet arrived, but the man I needed to see was in. He was sitting at his desk, reading the paper and enjoying a cigarette.

"I need a favor," I said.

George Loftus lowered his paper, but the cigarette still dangled out of his mouth, a thin line of smoke traveling upward. "Are you talking to me, Moses?"

I had expected this cool treatment. "George, I know what you are going to say. I couldn't get you out of the lockup any faster than I did. There was nothing I could have done to make your release happen any quicker."

He took a big drag off the smoke and exhaled in my general direction. "Where's your partner?"

"I can't use him on this. He's too new and there could be some shooting."

His eyebrows went straight up at the mention of gunfire. "You want me to help you with a situation where there might be shooting? Did Riley put you up to this joke?"

"No joke," I said. "Some guys are going to knock over a meat truck around ten this morning. We'll beat them to the location and get the drop on them. Shouldn't be too hard to avoid shooting."

"Did you tell that to Walker before that nut took his head off?"

Sam Walker, my last partner, had been shot gunned to death in a brothel by Christian Hanson. "That's a cruel blow, George."

He waved at me and put the cigarette out in an ashtray. "Sorry," he said. "I'll help you this time, Moses, but you're going to owe me big."

"That's a deal, George. Don't tell anyone where we are going, especially Keenan. I'll meet you in back at nine-thirty. We'll need a vehicle and two shotguns."

"I can manage that."

"By the way, the bad guys are crooked cops," I reached out and patted him on the shoulder. "Thanks, George."

He shook his head. "Just don't get me fucking killed."

I returned to my little desk just as Lieutenant Shipley happened to be walking by. He looked more tense than normal and he wasn't smiling, but he never smiled much anyway.

"I don't suppose you have anything to tell me that would make me feel better about my career as a police officer?"

"Lieutenant, what were you going to do before you became a cop?"

He thought for a moment. "I don't remember, Moses."

"I thought I was going to be a boxer so instead of getting my brains beat in mentally I'd be getting the shit pounded out of me physically. I wonder what is worse."

Shipley did manage a smile. "I'll take that to mean you have nothing informative to tell me."

"Sorry," I said.

"Things have cooled a bit, but I expect someone from either Headquarters or City Hall to call shortly. Think you can speed this along?"

"As soon as I have a suspect I will speed it along."

Shipley shook his head and walked down the aisle. I saw Keenan arrive, but he only waved and walked in the other direction. I rearranged a few files on my desk to make it look like I was busy while I waited to meet Loftus. I had about ten minutes to go when a clerk from downstairs came up to me and told me that Desk Sergeant Coogan had a call to put through to the detective's desk for me. I told him to put it through.

The desk phone only rang once when I picked it up. "This is Moses."

"Detective Moses," said a young girl's voice. "This is Patricia Farmer from St. Regina."

The girl who was worried about her grandmother being next. "Yes, Patricia."

"Is this a good time to talk to you?"

I saw movement to my right and noticed George Loftus headed for the rear exit. It would take him a few minutes to gather the weapons and locate a vehicle, but I didn't want him to wait long and get cold feet.

"This is not the best time. Can you call a little later?"

"I can come see you," she said. "When would be a good time for me to come into the precinct?"

If the meeting with Duvall and the crooked cops was on time, I really didn't see not being back here before noon. I hedged my bet a bit. "How about one o'clock?"

She hesitated. "I can be there at one."

"That's fine. Will one of your parents be coming with you?"

Another hesitation. "No. I need to talk to you alone with nobody else around."

This piqued my interest, but only mildly. Loftus was waiting. "Ask for me at the front desk, Patricia."

The line on the other end went dead. I looked for Keenan, but didn't see him. I got up to go find Loftus.

. . .

I had spent the day before sloshing around in water and mud because of the never ending torrent of rain we received. I spent a good part of time trying to clean a lot of the goop from my shoes. Soon after we arrived in the alley behind Farrell's Market I saw that all of my good work was for naught. The alley was nothing more but a muddy stream. Unless you wanted to go up onto some of the porches or roofs that backed up to it you were standing in slop.

Loftus took up a spot behind a small shed. He was about fifty yards from where I was, scrunched down behind a large garbage receptacle. The rain had definitely stopped, but the blazing sun and heat had returned. We weren't in that alley more than ten minutes and I was sweating. I looked at my watch. It was a little past ten. I got a little nervous, thinking this might be a replay of the night before.

At around ten-fifteen, I heard a good sized, horse drawn wagon making its way down the alley towards me. It drove right past me and I could see Roger Duvall driving the team that led it. It stopped right outside of the back entrance to Farrell's. Roger didn't move from his perch in the front of the wagon. He was waiting for something.

Not more than five minutes later an automobile entered the alley from the same direction as Duvall had. It was the same vehicle that Keenan and I had followed the day before. It pulled up right behind the wagon and two men got out. One was Daniel Bergman. The other was a short, tough looking guy. Duvall got off of his seat and came around the back of the wagon to meet them.

I couldn't tell what they were saying, but I didn't really need to know any more. Duvall lowered the back to the wagon and I could see a large, wooden crate. He stepped out of the way and Bergman and the other man stepped forward and started to go for the crate. I readied the shotgun and stepped into the alley, walking towards the wagon.

"What have we got here?" I said.

Bergman stepped forward and was about to draw his gun from the inside of his suitcoat when he saw the shotgun levelled at his chest. "What's this about, Moses?" he said.

"I'm not sure we've met, Bergman, unless you count the night that you and your friends jumped me."

"You're full of shit. You have no idea what you are talking about."

"As I said earlier, what is going on here?"

Bergman smiled. "My good friend here, Mr. Duvall, is making a very nice donation to the police department."

"That's not the way I see it or what we've heard from Duvall. This looks like a heist to me."

There was an eerie silence for just a moment. A moment too long. I couldn't see the other man who was almost directly behind Bergman. Apparently, Loftus couldn't see exactly what was going on or he would have seen the man draw his gun. The man's hand came up in a hurry and he fired two quick shots into the head of Roger Duvall. What followed was the roar of Loftus' shotgun as he blasted both barrels into the back of the other man. Both Duvall and the other man were dead before they splashed into the muddy alley.

Bergman had ducked a little, but never took his eye off my shotgun. I still had it pointed at him, but couldn't believe what had just happened. I walked closer to Bergman to look at Duvall. The right side of his head was blown away. He was dead. The other man was lying face down in several inches of water and mud. His back was a large red spot. He wasn't moving.

"Son of a fucking bitch," Loftus said. The barrels of his shotgun still smoking.

"On your knees," I told Bergman.

He got a concerned look on his face. "You gonna execute me right here, Moses?"

"No, you piece of shit. I'm going to arrest you."

He got down on his knees, but still kept his eyes on me. His arms were down at his side. Loftus came up behind him.

I raised the shotgun to his head level. "Hands behind your back."

Bergman put his hands behind his back and Loftus cuffed him.

I put the shotgun barrels under his chin. "Going to be tough to beat the robbery and extortion charges."

He smiled again. "Nobody had their weapons drawn, Moses. Mr. Duvall was coming around to open the wagon to make his donation. Nobody robbed or extorted anyone."

"That's not what Duvall told me," I said.

Bergman cocked his head towards the dead body of Roger Duvall. "Looks like Billy took care of your key witness."

I swallowed hard. "You don't think any of those taverns and bars you boosted yesterday will come forward and tell us what your payment scheme is with them?"

"I really don't think so."

I thought about Cora over at the Everleigh Club. I wasn't going to put her name out there and have her get similar treatment that Duvall got. "I think we'll find that sooner or later somebody will talk, and now we've got you for Duvall's murder."

Bergman laughed out loud. "Me? Not me, Moses. Billy Cogsdill shot Duvall and your man seems to have put Billy in the ground. This case is over with. As far as all the other garbage coming out of your mouth, I don't think you have a leg to stand on."

I was thinking of something to say when George Loftus used the butt of his shotgun and rammed Bergman in the back of the head. Bergman's eyes drifted up for a moment and then he fell face first into the muck.

Loftus looked disgusted by the whole episode. "He's just a piece of shit like you said. It was like you were arguing with a drunk, never getting anywhere." He stepped past me and headed towards the door for Farrell's"

"Where you going?"

"Gotta call this in. We need a wagon for the dead bodies and Bergman. I can't ride back with that shit in my vehicle."

• • • •

It took a while for the coroner's van to show up. It wasn't long after that when an arrest pickup van came for Daniel Bergman. He was defiant all the way back to the precinct and even down in lockup. He kept hollering that all they were doing was picking up a donation from Roger Duvall. He said that Loftus and I had broken up the meeting and provoked Billy Cogsdill into drawing his weapon. Most of his comments were directed at me. When he was being taken into the jail he yelled loudly that I was a murderer. Then there were remarks about how Jack Garfield was going to get me and he would be out of the jail in no time. I was relieved when I got upstairs and didn't have to listen to it anymore.

By the time I was back at my desk I had forgotten all about Patricia Farmer. In fact I was looking down at my shoes, and my pants cuffs, both ruined now by mud and water, when the call came from the front desk that I had a visitor. I was initially puzzled until my question was answered. It was Patricia Farmer.

The young girl was dressed in a simple, plain blue dress. I could tell by looking at the dress hem and her shoes that she hadn't walked very much to get here. There was no sign of mud or water on either item. When I first saw her, she looked agitated, nervous and maybe on the verge of tears. I had looked for Keenan when I first got in, but he wasn't around. Again, I leaned on George Loftus to sit in while I questioned her in one of the upstairs meeting rooms. George didn't complain this time because it might be a lead in the Old Lady Murders, as they were now being called.

Patricia was seated at the head of the table with George on one side of her and me on the other. We had given her a glass of water, but she didn't seem any calmer.

"Okay, Patricia, we'll get started," I said.

She nodded nervously and said nothing.

"You didn't bring either of your parents with you?"

She shook her head from side to side.

"I'm going to need you to answer verbally so Detective Loftus and I can keep an accurate record of this conversation."

"I don't want anyone, especially my parents or Sister Margaret, to know that I am here or what I am about to say," she answered slowly, but confidently.

I looked over at George, but he only shrugged.

"This conversation will be confidential just between us," I said, "but there may come a time, based on what you tell us, that your comments will have to become public."

She thought this over for a moment. Her eyes were looking straight ahead, trance like. As young as she was, I could tell she was going to be an attractive young woman, but now she resembled a scared rabbit. "I understand."

"The phone call that came into the precinct, the one that repeated what Lucy McLeod said about her father hating his grandmother, do you know who made it?"

Again there was that pause, eyes straight ahead, maybe nervousness, maybe fear. "I really can't have this get back to anyone that I was the one who told you any of this."

"Like I said earlier, we will do our best to keep this conversation confidential for the time being, but if any of what you tell us becomes material to our case, your comments may have to become public."

"She's a good friend of mine, my closest friend," she blurted out. "I don't want to see her get in any trouble."

"We're just trying to find out why she called into the precinct. We are trying to find out who is killing these women."

She nodded slowly. "At first, I thought she was trying to help you catch the killer. We all heard Lucy make that comment and we had seen Mr. McLeod. There is something a little strange about him. We thought that maybe if he hated his grandmother, he might be behind the murders."

"So if this person had this thought that maybe he was behind the murders and she made this call to the precinct to help us, she won't get into that much trouble. We'd just like to talk with her."

"That's what I thought at first. I'm not so sure anymore."

"What aren't you sure about?" George asked.

"Wait a minute. Was this girl at the meeting we had a St. Regina with all the girls?" I asked.

She shook her head. "She couldn't be there that day."

"Answer Detective Loftus' question," I said.

A large, single tear rolled out of her left eye and ran all the way down to her chin. "I think she knows something about the killer. I think she knows who the killer is."

"Then why call us and tell us a story about Gavin McLeod?" George asked.

"To possibly take away any possibility that you might look at the real killer."

"And how do you know that she feels this way?" I asked.

She shrugged. "Little comments that she's made. Nothing complete, mind you. Just little statements."

"What is this girl's name?"

She closed her eyes and took an enormous, deep breath, exhaling loudly. "Her name is Madeline Marsden. She is my best friend."

On the way to visit Madeline Marsden, we ran into Keenan in the hallway. The look on his face told me that he was upset about something and I knew that it was probably me.

"Why didn't you tell me about the meeting with Roger Duvall this morning?" His face was beet red.

"I got a tip and when it was time to go I looked for you. You weren't around. We didn't have a lot of time so I grabbed Loftus to go with me."

He mulled this over for a few seconds. "And this meeting with the

Farmer girl?"

"Same thing. She showed up and you were nowhere to be found. I asked George to sit in. Where the hell were you anyway?"

The color in his face hadn't lessened. "I had to go to Headquarters," he said hurriedly.

"Why would you need to do that?"

"I have asked for a transfer. I do not believe that working in homicide is right for me."

I nodded. I wasn't sure he could handle homicide much longer. I was more than sure that he couldn't work with me. "George and I have a lead on the Old Lady Murders. We have to get going."

"I was told to stay here and help with administrative assignments until my transfer was finalized. I informed Shipley of this. I'm no longer working with you on this case."

"And the case involving Daniel Bergman and other detectives who work with Jack Garfield?"

I didn't think his face could get any redder, but it did. "I have spoken to no one about that."

"It won't matter anyway," I said and I turned to go down the stairs.

• • •

Madeline Marsden and her family lived on Indiana Street which was located a little west of Prairie Avenue where all of the wealthy types of the city had residences. You wouldn't look at the houses on Indiana and say that the people that lived in them were poor. They just weren't as elite as the houses on Prairie. The Marsdens lived in a conservative looking, two story house. The lawn and the shrubs that fronted the property were all in good shape; not one little weed was showing in the grass. We had asked Patricia Farmer where Madeline lived and she had given us the address. It had been easy for her. She lived right across the street and we saw her on her porch as we moved to ring the doorbell. As George hit the button I looked across the street. Patricia had gone inside.

The door was answered by a plump, little woman in a conservative house dress. She had a round face with a head full of tight, brown curls. She also had on rather thick spectacles. She wore a look of concern when we introduced ourselves, but we were used to that.

"We'd like to speak to your daughter, Madeline," I said.

"What is this about?" she asked. "Has she done anything wrong?"

"That's what we want to ask her about. It's important that we speak to her right away."

"I see," she said.

"Is Mr. Marsden around?"

"He is in St. Louis on business. He won't return home for another day or so."

"We really need to speak with Madeline."

She asked us nicely to have a seat in her living room. The curtains were drawn on all of the windows, but it was still hot in the room. George sat in a well cushioned Queen Anne's chair; I sat on the sofa.

"I need a chair like this, Moses," George said. "You can sit in it and you know your ass isn't going to hit the floor."

"That's important, George."

Loftus smiled, but knew I wasn't in the frame of mind to joke about anything.

Mrs. Marsden returned several minutes with a young girl that was a younger version of her mother. Same body shape, same round face and I was pretty sure the same type of eye glasses. "Madeline," her mother said, "these men are with the police. They would like to ask you a few questions."

Madeline smiled at us and said nothing.

"Madeline, we were at your school the other day and asked some of the other girls in the Daughters of the City what they knew about a comment the Lucy McLeod made about her father not liking his grandmother. Do you know what comment I am talking about?"

"Yes," Madeline said quietly.

"What did you think about it when Lucy made that remark?"

Madeline's eyes lacked any recognition of the fact that she might be in trouble. She didn't seem nervous or upset in any way that the police were in her living room and asking about a murder investigation. "I thought what Lucy said was a little scary. I knew that a couple of old women had been murdered. Lucy said that her father hated his grandmother. The thought occurred to me that maybe Mr. McLeod was taking out this hatred on these old women. I thought that maybe he was involved in the murders."

"Just because of what she had said about her father?"

"Yes."

"So what did you do about it?"

She didn't blink. "I made a call to your precinct office and repeated what Lucy had said about her father. I disguised my voice, but I thought I was pretty clear in what I said."

Mrs. Marsden let out a small gasp of air. "Madeline!" she exclaimed.

"I thought it might help you," she said. "I read my father's copy of the *Tribune* and it said the police had very little in the way of leads or evidence. I was just trying to help."

"No one put you up to this? You acted alone?" George asked. He was sitting up, not leaning back in the Queen Anne's chair.

"No one put me up to anything," she said.

"Do you have any idea who might have sent two drawings over to the precinct?" I asked.

She turned to look at me with her emotionless eyes. "I don't know anything about any drawings or who might have sent them."

I looked over a George, but he had slumped back into the chair. Madeline had admitted to making the call that led us to look at Gavin McLeod, but that was it. There didn't seem much more to it. A thirteen year old girl heard something that she thought could help the police. She just went about telling us about it in the wrong way. I thought about what Patricia Farmer had said about Madeline knowing something about the killer, but that seemed farfetched.

"Is there anything else that you would like to tell us?" I asked.

She thought quietly for a moment, unblinking. "I don't believe so."

Madeline's mother looked stunned, but we thanked Madeline and her for their time and headed back to the precinct.

"Strange girl," I said to Loftus.

"She was talking to us, but it was like she wasn't there," Loftus said.

With the arrest of Daniel Bergman and the murder of Roger Duvall, followed by the shooting of Billy Cogsdill, my day had started on a bit of a dubious note. With the interviews with both Patricia Farmer and Madeline Marsden, the day had taken a strange turn. I wasn't sure which way to go with what we learned from both girls, if anything. When we got back to the precinct I was told that I was in immediate demand in Lieutenant Shipley's office. This could only mean that my day was about to get worse.

Shipley was sitting behind his desk and was staring straight ahead. His look reminded me a bit of the look on Madeline Marsden's face. Like he wasn't there, Loftus had said. I knocked lightly on the door and his head quickly snapped in my direction.

"I heard that you wanted to see me, Lieutenant."

"Moses, I need some answers from you right now."

Shipley had not said hello. "Answers pertaining to what?"

"Well, "he said, "I think we should start with the Old Lady Murders. After the little stunt that you and Loftus pulled this morning, I have had several calls from Headquarters. Some people down there would really like to know what you are doing."

I felt a hot flash run up the back of my neck. "When you say little stunt, are you referring to the arrest of Daniel Bergman?"

"That might be a good place to start."

"I'm pretty sure that Bergman is involved in a pretty wide scale extortion scheme. What we witnessed this morning was the theft of a crate of steaks by Detective Bergman and his partner, Billy Cogsdill. They were extorting meat shipments by blackmailing the driver Roger Duvall. We caught them red-handed and for some reason Cogsdill shot Duvall and George shot Cogsdill. Pretty clear cut to me."

"Except that Detective Bergman says that Duvall was making a donation of the steaks to the department."

"That is the most preposterous thing that I have ever heard and we can easily squash all of that by talking to the owners of the meat packing company."

"Bergman said he had no knowledge how Duvall got the steaks and had no knowledge that they might be stolen."

"That's another lie, Lieutenant."

"Well, Captain Garfield and a troop of lawyers are on their way down here to bail Bergman out. I was told that Garfield is not very happy with us, particularly you."

"He doesn't like me very much." I didn't bother to go into to the tavern extortion I had witnessed or the possible case involving Stanley Kerjewski and Cora from The Everleigh Club.

"It doesn't do you or any of us any good to continue to make enemies at Headquarters. Garfield is already sure you were behind the death of your father and Amos Stokes."

"This case has a lot of arms. I'm going to find out how far it reaches."

"I can't help you, Moses, if they suspend you. I'm advising you to leave it alone."

"Point taken. Anything else, Lieutenant?"

Shipley smiled. "Aren't we forgetting something like maybe the Old Lady Murders? If you have forgotten them, you are the only one. Headquarters is convinced that you are doing very little on this case."

I rolled my shoulders to loosen some of the tension that had built up. "In my defense, we have very little to work with. On the positive side, we are starting to get little bits of information that should lead us to the killer."

Now Shipley smiled. "Do you want me to believe that little line?"

"It wasn't a lie. "It's how I feel."

"Then, by all means, I will report that you are closing in on the murderer. Would that be an accurate statement?"

I wondered for a second how long I wanted to continue this line of the conversation. "I think that would be accurate."

"Then, that is what I will report. Anything else?"

"I understand Mr. Coughlin will no longer be assisting me."

"You understand correctly. It seems he didn't care for seeing grandmothers suffocated with their own pillows. He also wasn't in agreement with some of your rogue investigations. Your conduct made him nervous."

"Well, that's fine. As long as were tattling on each other, I believe he may be a snitch. I think he told some people where I was going to be one night and on another occasion he tipped someone off that we were on to them. That behavior was making me nervous."

Shipley's mouth hung open for a bit, digesting what I had told him. "I can only tell you, Moses, that you should steer clear of any interaction with Captain Garfield or any of his men for the foreseeable future. I think that would be in your best interest."

"Thank you for looking after my interests, Lieutenant."

• • •

The usually dry chicken at Cooper's was dryer than normal. I wasn't particularly hungry so all I managed to do was push the chicken and carrots around the plate with my fork. My lack of hunger didn't include my thirst. The first couple of whiskeys went down a little too easy. I caught myself, thinking of the hazards of getting drunk and trying to navigate my way safely to my apartment. This thought made me pause and I sipped my third drink.

I wouldn't describe being tormented as the way I felt, but it was close. The so called lead that we got from Patricia Farmer about Madeline Marsden and the precinct phone call didn't turn out to be much. Madeline had taken something she heard and called it in to us. She had made an immature decision and that was that.

When you deduct the phone call we are left with the drawings of Mrs. Gilford and her unfortunate cat. There is no mistaking that the killer drew these sketches. The coincidence that they came in the same day as Madeline's phone call bothers me, but I think it is just that, a coincidence. When you look at the phone call, which yielded nothing, and the pictures, that is all we have. Lieutenant Shipley is right to be frustrated by the case and its progression. That's the problem. There is little progression.

My private little war with Captain Garfield, and his friends, is not over. I know they were behind blackmailing Stanley. We had talked with Roger Duvall and they definitely had him going in their direction. This got Duvall killed. I didn't witness Daniel Bergman squeezing any of the bar owners directly, but his behavior that morning had all the makings of it. I knew with a little leg work I could confirm what was going on. I was also pretty sure Keenan had warned somebody about the meeting with Cora. That meeting never came off. There was some stuff here that needed looking into. My problem here was that Shipley had told me to back off. The bigger problem was how I interpreted his order.

Captain Jack Garfield still had it in for me. He was convinced that I was behind the death of my father and Amos Stokes. How he had pieced either of these two cases together was a mystery to me. Why he cared so much about the two dead louses was another story. Garfield would step up his investigation of me. I was interested in what he would find.

I finished my whiskey, paid the bill, and was on my way home thinking I had gone through every troubling thing I could imagine. That was until I got to my building. It was past nine and Lois Winston was sitting alone on the porch, smoking a cigarette. It suddenly occurred to me that Lois was another kind of mystery. And then I thought of her boy, Freddie. He had seen Christian Hanson up close. That sent a chill up my back.

"Good evening, Detective Moses," Lois said. "It's such a nice night out, I thought I would sit out here for a bit before I went to bed."

It was a beautiful night. The rain from the day before had cleared the air and the moon was shining brightly above us. "Hello, Lois. It is a wonderful night."

"I saw you made the papers again. The late edition *Tribune* said that you were involved in an early morning shootout."

"An unfortunate matter," I said. "Hopefully, that fine newspaper got it right and said that I was not involved in any gunplay."

"It said someone shot a street thug and your Detective Loftus shot that man."

I wouldn't identify Roger Duvall as a street thug, but I let it pass. "Is my little friend Freddie doing okay?"

In the dark I could make out Lois exhaling smoke in my direction. "Actually, he's a bit scared. He didn't like the looks of those men who came looking for you the other night."

"Tell him not to worry. Those men have business with me. They're not involved in hurting children."

"Nevertheless, I keep my gun near me at all times."

"Ah, the gun that saved my life when Annie Oakley started firing away."

She laughed. "You have to say it was very handy that night."

"That it was. What made you get a firearm anyway?"

"The first reason was when William disappeared. I feel, for certain, that he got involved with some bad people and he ended up owing them money. When he was gone, I thought they might come and pay Freddie and me a visit. I got the gun for that."

"And the second reason?"

"Well, you know, Detective Moses. This is the city and it's not all that civilized. It is purely for protection."

"But you lived in the city before."

She laughed again. "That little house that we had was like living in the country. We were so removed from the hustle and bustle that it really seems that way."

I nodded and noticed what seemed like a shooting star in the sky. "What are some of the things that you miss most about being away from your old house?"

"Really just some of the quiet and not having to worry about what Freddie is up to every minute."

I thought of my two children, who had died in the Iroquois Theatre Fire. Was I ever worried about them? It seemed so long ago.

"Are you getting anywhere on your Old Lady Murders?"

I sighed. "Not far enough. I feel like the fisherman who has been out on his boat all day and has nothing but a few nibbles to show for his effort."

"Gets a little frustrating I would imagine."

My earlier word was tormenting. "You could say that."

"Hey, Detective Moses, I have to ask you a little favor."

The woman had saved my life and I liked little Freddie. "If I can help you I will."

"I might not have used the best discretion in bringing a man home the other night. It's no excuse, but it was purely a weakness on my part."

I thought of prostitutes, whiskey and opium. "We all have them," I said.

"I just wanted to ask you to forgive me and to not think less of me for my actions."

"You don't have to ask for my forgiveness and I don't think anything less of you. Like I said, we all make decisions that aren't always the best."

"Yeah, you're right," she said. "You're a good man, Detective Moses."

I hadn't had that said about me in a long time. It made me feel good.

I went to bed and I thought about Lois Winston. She was a beautiful woman, trying to raise a young boy on her own. I liked Lois. Even with the mystery of her husband, I thought I would like to get to know her better. She had been nice to me, but had shown little as far as interest in me. Maybe all I needed to do was ask. What was the worst thing I would find out?

*****

August 14th

It was unusual to get to the precinct and find that you had a telephone message. It was extremely unusual to find that you had two of them, but that was what Sergeant Coogan said to me when I entered the building. Surprisingly, I had slept pretty well and I felt good. Maybe my little conversation with Lois had given me some peace, but I didn't get a lot of time to reflect on it.

"Two telephone messages?" I said.

"Two people called for you," Coogan said. "I wrote down the names and the return numbers."

He handed me two little pieces of paper. One of the callers was Stanley Kerjewski. The other was Judge Robert Burke, James' father. This was the boy who saw "two angels" near Agnes Gilford's house around the time she was murdered. I took the easy one and decided to call Stanley back first. There was a telephone in the first floor conference room. I made the call there.

"Hello, Patrick," Stanley said after his secretary tracked him down. I have a bit of information for you."

"Been behaving yourself, Stanley?"

He lowered his voice. "I've been good, Patrick. I'm trying."

"That's probably not a bad idea, at least for the time being. What kind of information do you have for me?"

"It may or not mean anything, but it could be the reason that Jack Garfield continues to investigate you."

"What is it, Stanley?"

"It appears that Captain Jack had a very close friend when they were in the police academy together. They remained close friends from then until one of them died."

"You are going to tell me?"

"Sure. Garfield's close friend was Thomas Morgan."

I took a deep breath and thought for a moment.

"Your Thomas Morgan, Patrick. This is the same man that you shot to death when you found out he was helping Simon Kluge remove prostitutes from the street."

It made sense now. I'd never met Garfield and couldn't imagine why he had such hatred for me. "But Morgan was helping Kluge."

"Apparently that doesn't get you off of the list of biggest bastards according to Garfield. For whatever reason he feels the need to vindicate Morgan through finding something on you."

"He won't find anything on me, Stanley, and I doubt if he'll be hassling you much either. We're going to turn the heat up on Garfield and his crew very soon, as soon as I can."

"I appreciate that, Patrick, but be very careful. I have heard that Garfield is a very vengeful person."

I didn't need to be reminded of this. I wasn't sure how far I would get pushing an internal investigation of Garfield, but I was damned if I was going to let him charge me with any crimes. I smiled. Maybe we could just call it all a tie and move on.

My second call was to Judge Robert Burke. The number he had given was to the courthouse and his chambers. I had to wait again as a clerk went to find him.

"Judge Burke," said a serious voice after a few minutes wait.

"Judge, this is Detective Patrick Moses. I am returning the call you made earlier this morning."

"I am glad that you called me back, Detective. I have something to tell you about the murder of Agnes Gilford."

Now I was all ears. "Please go ahead, sir."

"You remember when my son, James, said that he had seen two angels around the Gilford home?"

"I do," I said.

"James came to me in my study last evening. He gave me a copy of a program from an Easter pageant we had seen back in the spring. When he gave it to me he said two angels again."

"Do you have any idea what he is referring to?"

"I think I do, yes. In the pageant, there was a parade of angels. After the show James went over where the girls who played the angels were standing. He was talking with them and they were joking around with him. I think James recognized two of the angels from the pageant. I think that's who he saw by Mrs. Gilford's house."

"This pageant. Where did it take place?"

"At St. Regina's."

$\bullet$ $\bullet$ $\bullet$

My heart was racing when I got off the telephone with Judge Burke. I walked out of the little meeting room and almost ran right into Jack Garfield. His face was flushed red and there were beads of sweat on the sides of his face and forehead.

"Detective Moses! I assume this is fate pulling the two of us together at this time."

"Captain, I am very busy at this time. I can't be talking to you about your theories on my criminal behavior."

"Step in here for one second, Moses."

He walked past me and into the room that I had just vacated. I could give him a minute, no more. I followed.

"Close the door, son," he said. I wasn't close to his son, but I closed the door anyway.

He took a deep breath and wiped away the sweat on his face. "I don't know what you think you are up to with all of these accusations you made to Detective Bergman. I don't care how far you try to reach to try and turn this around to make me and my men look like we are the guilty ones, but it won't work. No one is going to believe you. You are the one that is guilty here, Moses. You are the one in trouble. I know this and I will stop at nothing to prove it."

His face was getting redder and sweat was back in all of the same spots. When he spoke spittle had flown in my direction. "I appreciate your persistence, Captain."

He looked flabbergasted. "What did you say, Moses?"

"In a nice way, I guess I said fuck you, and if you don't have any real reason to hold me I need to be gone from here." Without waiting for his answer, I left the room.

•   •   •

As always, Harold Pinter was busy in his little office, staring down at something on his desk. I knocked and he looked up. "Ah, Patrick, are you keeping busy." He smiled.

"It seems like since I have been back like I have stepped into a beehive of activity."

"Anything good coming of it?"

"Not much so far, but we're getting there."

"The Old Lady Murders? How can I help?"

"The sketches that were sent over to us. Do you still have them here?"

"Of course," he said, getting up from his desk. He moved slowly to a small table on the other side of the room. I followed. The two drawings were spread out on the table.

"Were you looking for anything particular?" Harold asked.

"That's just it. What about the pictures stood out? I'm looking for something that might be a characteristic of this artist."

"That's too easy, Patrick. It's right here," he said pointing.

My eyes followed his finger. It was right above the head of Agnes Gilford. "I'm not sure what you are pointing out."

"It's the artist's use of the pencil. Take a look a Mrs. Gilford's hair, her eyebrows and her finger nails. Here the artist has really bore down on the pencil, giving the impression that those areas are all extremely dark. We know that Mrs. Gilford's hair was gray or silver; her nails had no coloring on them at all.

"You can see it as well on the cat in the other picture. The eye balls are totally black as are the nails on the animal. I'm not sure why, but the artist likes to accentuate certain areas with darker shades of the pencil. Definitely hair color, areas around the eye and nails."

I nodded slowly. "Was there anything else?"

"I'm not an art expert, so forgive me for coming up with so little."

"I didn't mean it that way. I just wondered if you noticed anything else."

Harold smiled. "From the strokes of the pencil that drew Mrs. Gilford's hair, I would say the artist is left handed."

• • •

I could tell by the look on her face that Sister Margaret was growing wary of seeing us. Regardless, she invited us into her office and shut the door behind her as she came around her desk and sat down. The room was hot, but Sister Margaret looked cool in her habit. I was hot and I'm sure Loftus wasn't feeling much better.

"You had a pageant that you ran here at Easter time," I said. "I understand that there were several angels in the pageant that were played by girls from your school."

She shifted uneasily in her chair. "We run that pageant every year at Easter," she said.

"It's not the pageant I care about so much. It's a list of the girls who played the angels."

She got up slowly and moved to a cabinet on her left. She sifted through some papers in the top drawer and came out with a small pamphlet. It looked like a show program. "What would you like to know?"

"Just the name of the angels in the show."

She looked down and read slowly. "Mary Beth Ayers, Samantha Boyd, Madeline Marsden and Patricia Farmer."

"Son of a bitch," I said.

"Detective Moses," Sister Margaret said.

"Sorry," I said. My stomach tightened and I heard Loftus groan. "Those girls are nowhere around here today?"

"Not today, Detective."

"That's okay. I wonder if I could ask you another question about these four girls."

"You can ask me anything. I'm not sure I can answer all of your questions."

"Of these four girls, can you tell me if any of them have any particular artistic talents?"

She stood up and asked us to follow her. We left her office and headed in the direction of the main entrance of the school. Near the entrance, on the hall walls, was an exhibit of drawings. As I got closer I could see that all of the drawings were of President Teddy Roosevelt. Most were clearly amateurish; some were better. A few stood out. Sister Margaret had stopped in front of one of these.

The drawing she was looking at showed the fiery president as he was in the middle of some impassioned speech. His one finger was raised as if making a point. The nail on the finger was a deep black. The President's eye brows, mustache and hair were all black. I stepped closer and could see that the artist had placed her initials in the lower right corner of the drawing. A very clear PF was shown there.

"Patricia Farmer is a very talented artist," Sister Margaret said. "She prefers to work with pencils and she has been known to sketch just about anything."

I thought of the open book of drawings at the murder scene. Patricia had been there and had been looking through that book. She had been at all three scenes, enjoying cake and cookies at two others.

"Do you know much about her friendship with Madeline Marsden?" I asked.

She thought for a moment. "An odd couple, for sure. I've seen the two of them together and it still amazes me. Most of the time Madeline is very silent; Patricia seems to be doing all the talking. When they walk around the school Patricia is usually three steps in front of Madeline. Madeline seems to follow her around like a little dog."

Not only was my stomach tightening, but my heart was racing, beating quicker as we learned more.

"What does all of this about the pageant angels and Patricia's art work have to do with anything?" she asked.

"Right now, I'm not sure," I said. "I hope nothing."

• • •

We decided to wait until evening to visit the homes of Patricia Farmer and Madeline Marsden. We wanted both sets of parents to be there if possible. It was decided that Riley O'Donnell, George Loftus, Harold Pinter and myself would do the interviews. I was going to lead the team. The first house we were going to go to was the Farmer residence. Patricia seemed to be the leader of the twosome from what Sister Margaret told us. We wanted to get her story first. It was also decided that we would interview each girl separately and not let either of the girls know what the other had said.

It was one of those August nights where there is a hint of heat still in the air, but it is not oppressive. Some of the humidity lingers, but not enough to make you sweat. You get the feeling that the hottest days of summer are over and fall is around the corner. Most of that would be peaceful for the affluent neighborhood the two girls lived in. The sight of three police vehicles pulling up in front of the Farmer residence with four detectives filing out of them surely caused the neighbors to wonder. We went up the stairs of the house and rang the doorbell.

When Cynthia Farmer answered the door we could see where her daughter got her good looks. Cynthia was tall, blonde and very attractive. Her husband, Joe, was a tall man as well, with a receding hairline and a five o'clock shadow.

"May I help you?" Cynthia asked.

I showed my badge and introduced only myself. "We would like to have a word with your daughter, Patricia."

Joe Farmer stepped in front of his wife in the doorway. "Why do you want to talk to Patricia?" There was a little tough guy, arrogance to his voice, but I took it only as a concerned father.

"We think she may have been involved in a crime and we would like to talk with her. Now would be a good time."

He looked past me at the other three. "You need four officers to question a thirteen year old girl?"

"We don't want to miss anything," I said. "Now, may we come in or should we do this in the precinct?"

The Farmers let us in and we were led to a nice living room with two large windows. When you looked outside you could see the neighbors milling about, some pointing fingers. Joe Farmer went to get Patricia. Cynthia Farmer closed the curtains in the room, taking a good part of the light out of it. We all remained standing. Cynthia sat on the couch.

When Joe returned with Patricia we asked them to all be seated.

Patricia took a seat between her parents. Her face showed nothing, maybe disinterest. We had planned this out in the office. Harold stepped forward with the picture of the tortured Agnes Gilford. He held it out for Patricia to see. I heard Cynthia gasp at the sight of the drawing.

"Patricia," I said, "are you the person who drew this sketch?"

Patricia looked at the picture as if she was really considering whether it was her work. Her face showed no emotion, no fear, barely a hint that anything was wrong. "Yes," she said.

"What is that a picture of?" Joe asked. His face was fraught with anxiety; Cynthia's eyes were moving from the picture to her daughter, to us and then back to the picture.

"There have been three murders of older women in the city in the past month. The papers call them crudely The Old Lady Murders. This drawing that your daughter has made is of the latest victim, Agnes Gilford. We have a strong reason to believe that Patricia was in Mrs. Gilford's house at the time of the murder."

Cynthia Farmer gasped again, this time loudly. Her head came forward into her hands and she began to cry. Joe Farmer stood quickly, defensively. George Loftus came up behind me and placed a hand on Joe's shoulder. He sat back down. "This can't be, Detective," Joe said. "Patricia is an Honor Student and she helps with the Daughters of the City." Patricia's eyes looked straight away.

"Patricia," I said. "Please tell us how you came to draw this sketch and the one of the cat."

Harold stepped forward and produced the second drawing of the cat hanging from the chandelier.

"My god," Joe said. Cynthia was bawling loudly, out of control.

Patricia raised her eyes and looked at me. My first thought was that I had asked her something simple like who the President was. "I drew her after Madeline had tied her up. I drew the picture of the cat after Madeline had hanged the cat from the light."

"Patricia, no," Joe said. The look on his face showed shock, disbelief. His wife continued to cry.

I took a deep breath. "How did you know that Mrs. Gilford was going to be alone?"

"We heard it after mass one Sunday. The family was going on a trip out east. She was going to be all alone. We knew she would let two girls in who offered to help her out with some chores. We told her that Mr. Gilford had asked us to stop by. It was very simple to get in the house."

I didn't feel right. Her demeanor was making me wonder what type of person I was talking to. "And how did you gain access to the first two women that were killed?"

She peered deep into my eyes. I was frightened for a moment. She smiled a little. "We were there with the Daughters of the City. We knocked on the doors and told the women we were there to help them again. They were old and feeble. I don't think they knew any better. They let us right in. It was easy."

Now Joe Farmer was crying. The monster daughter sat between her two parents as calm as could be. I had never seen anything like it.

"How did you go about what you did?" I noticed that my hands had started to shake a bit. Riley said he needed a smoke and left the room. Loftus was groaning with every word Patricia uttered. Harold had his eyes down, his feet doing a pace without going anywhere.

"That was very easy, as well," she said. "All three women let us in easily. I told them I would read to them while Madeline started some chores. They all seemed to like that. We got them to sit in a chair and I started to read to them from books or any papers that were lying about. It was at this time that Madeline cut up the sheets. When she was done she would come up behind the women and loop a strip of sheet around them. She had them tied to those chairs in seconds."

"They didn't fight back at all?" I asked.

Patricia shrugged. "Madeline is surprisingly strong. She was able to hold them down while she got the binds around them. It didn't take long."

I glanced at both parents. They had been overwhelmed to hear their daughter's confession. Cynthia was sobbing, eyes closed, head down; Joe looked straight ahead, eyes brimming with tears, clearly in shock.

"Why did you gag the women?"

"That's too clear, isn't it? They saw us, knew who we were."

"But when you gagged them and stuffed the pillow pieces into their mouths you choked them. You cut off their ability to breathe."

Patricia's face was still clear of any reaction to the whole conversation. A thought occurred to me that I should slap her.

"These old women had been sick," she said. "We had heard there was suffering. We were just trying to help them with their pain."

"Oh, Jesus," George Loftus said loudly.

We had no knowledge of any illness issue with the three dead women. "Why kill Mrs. Gilford's cat?"

She smiled. "Mrs. Gilford wouldn't die. Madeline hanged the cat with the thought that the shock might do it. She was right."

Listening to this teenage girl describe these murders was almost worse than seeing the carved up prostitutes from the winter before.

"So," I continued, "you thought by killing these women you were easing them from their pain. That was why you committed these crimes?"

"Not at first. Madeline talked so much about how bored she was this summer. She talked about it so much, I finally agreed with her. Madeline wanted to do something to break the boredom. Madeline came up with the idea to commit a crime that the police would struggle to solve. We left almost no clues. At the same time we felt like we were helping the women."

"But the pictures you sent. Those were pretty good clues. Someone was going to find out who drew them."

Again, that slight shrug. "That was my idea. I thought Madeline was going a bit too far. I thought it was time to end the game."

The game, I thought. These girls thought this was a game. Riley returned to the room. I knew he had four daughters. He was probably wondering what would become of them in the coming years.

"Riley," I said, "will you take Patricia out to your vehicle and sit with her while George, Harold and I visit Madeline Marsden's house?"

"I can do that, Patrick," Riley said quietly.

"Patricia Farmer, we are arresting you for the murders of Grace Muldor, Dorothy Casson and Agnes Gilford." At those words, Cynthia Farmer sat up, gasped loudly and fainted. She fell backward against the couch. Patricia looked up at me and smiled.

Harold was able to get Cynthia revived and we left her with her husband while Riley led Patricia to one of our waiting vehicles. The number of on looking neighbors had grown but nobody said anything as Patricia was placed inside the vehicle.

"Notice anything odd about that whole interrogation?" I asked.

"You're kidding, right, Moses?" George asked. "The whole fucking thing was odd."

"She takes no responsibility for any of it," Harold said. "Every thought, every action was carried out by Madeline Marsden. Other than drawing the sketches, all Patricia Farmer did was tag along and witness the whole thing."

"Precisely," I said, looking across the street. "Let's go see what Madeline thinks. When we met her I didn't get the impression that we were with a heartless killer."

• • •

It didn't take us long to get to Madeline Marsden. As we began to cross the street we saw Madeline and her mother, Sally, standing on their porch, watching everything unfold on Patricia Farmer. I looked at Madeline and when our eyes connected she left her mother's side and started down her steps towards us, her startled mother trailing her. She came up to us just as we had crossed the street.

"What are you doing to Patricia?" she asked. She was wearing a very plain brown dress and her thick eyeglasses.

"We are going to take her into the precinct and ask her a few questions," I said.

"I told you I made that phone call," she said loudly. She was almost yelling at me.

Her mother came up quickly. "Detective Moses, what is going on?"

"Mrs. Marsden, has your husband returned from his business trip?"

"He has not. He is still in St. Louis."

The neighbors had begun to circle us from both sides. "I suggest we go into your house. I don't think you want to have this discussion right out on the lawn."

"What discussion is that?" she asked.

"I did it all," Madeline said loudly. "Patty did nothing."

"What are you talking about, Maddie?" her mother asked.

"Into the house," I said, and I grabbed Madeline by the elbow and turned her towards their house. There were a couple of grumbles from the crowd, but I heard Loftus quiet them. I got Madeline up the stairs and into their living room. Harold was behind me with Mrs. Marsden who hadn't stopped talking. Loftus followed us all into the house. I sat Madeline on one of the Queen Anne's chairs.

"Will someone please tell me what is going on?" Sally Marsden said. She had taken the seat in the chair next to her daughter.

"Mrs. Marsden, we have reason to believe that Madeline and Patricia Farmer have been involved in the deaths of three older women. As a matter of fact, we feel the two of them are our prime suspects."

"Deaths," she said softly.

"More like murders," Loftus said. I gave him a look. He only shrugged.

"Madeline, what are these men saying? Tell me this can't be true."

Suddenly, like turning on an electric switch, Madeline wore the frozen face we had seen before. It took on some of the features of a zombie, looking straight ahead, eyes glazed.

"Madeline, are you alright?" I asked.

"Patricia only wanted to scare them," Madeline said. "I tied them up. I put the pillow stuffing in their mouths and gags over their noses. I gagged them. They needed that help to finally relieve them of their pain. I could see that."

"Oh my God," Sally said, covering her mouth with her hands.

"Patricia just wanted to scare them. I was the one who did everything else."

"Didn't you think you would be eventually caught?" I asked. "When you called the precinct and left those drawings there, didn't you think that would lead us to you?"

"The call was to mislead you," she said calmly and then her eyes blinked rapidly and she looked at me. "What pictures?"

"The ones that Patricia drew of Agnes Gilford and her cat. You knew she drew them. Didn't you know that she anonymously dropped them off at the precinct?"

She swallowed hard, taking this information in and then her eyes returned to the dead-eyed glare. "That doesn't matter. Patricia wanted to scare them. She drew a few pictures. I did everything else."

"This is too simple," George said.

"Madeline, you are under arrest for the murders of Grace Muldor, Dorothy Casson and Agnes Gilford. You will come with us now."

Madeline rose without another word being spoken. George began to lead her down the stairs into one of the other waiting vehicles.

"Where are you taking her?" Sally Marsden asked.

"She will be held in the Twenty-Second Precinct building until the time that she is arraigned."

"She won't be able to come home tonight?"

The woman was clearly in shock. "That's not going to be possible, Mrs. Marsden."

She looked out the window at the crowd of her neighbors, watching her daughter being led into a police vehicle. "How did this happen?" she said. "She's a very good student, belongs to the Daughters of the City, and loves her garden in the back yard. She wouldn't do anything like this. This wouldn't have happened if she hadn't started spending time with the Farmer girl. Her father is going to be very upset."

I nodded. "We have to go now. Perhaps you should try and contact your husband."

I left the house and the poor mother, mumbling to herself in the living room. Both of the girls had been taken to separate autos which would be driven by Riley and George. Harold and I would lead the way in the first vehicle. As I walked past the car that held Patricia Farmer I could see her clearly in the back seat. She turned to look at me and she smiled broadly. Then she waved at me with her left hand. Again there was a pitch in my stomach and a chill ran up my back.

"She's smiling," Harold said, behind me.

"This is an extremely bizarre case and these are two extremely unusual girls."

"I'm not sure prosecuting the two of them will be so easy."

I opened my door and slid onto the seat. Harold got in beside me. I didn't respond to his comment. Something told me that he was right.

The two girls would be held in the cells of the precinct until we had time to present our case to the District Attorney and arraignment was set. Luckily, there were two free cells away from each other and anyone else where the girls were held. We didn't want them talking with each other or anyone else. Time was precious as we were sure they would lawyer up soon and they had good money. They would have good lawyers and the legal shit storm would start. My stomach already ached.

• • •

It was getting late by the time the two girls were processed and I was about to leave the precinct when Lieutenant Shipley came by my desk. It was first time I had ever seen him out of full uniform. He looked relaxed and was smiling.

"You in a good mood, Lieutenant?" I asked.

"I hope so, Moses. Headquarters and City Hall are happy with the arrests. A bit confused but happy."

"Confused?"

"When word got to them that two thirteen year old girls had been arrested for the murders I believe there was quite a bit of confusion. It's not your run of the mill arrest."

"No, it's not." I stood, ready to leave.

Shipley placed his hand on my arm. "These arrests are good, aren't they Moses?"

"As much as I wanted to believe that what I was hearing was make believe, I couldn't. Those two girls killed those three women. One of them said it was because the women were sick and they wanted to relieve them of their pain. She also said they were bored with summer. It's an unbelievable tale, but it is accurate. The arrests are good, but it should be a hell of a trial."

"God help us," Shipley said as I started for the downward stairs.

• • •

I walked outside and found a brilliantly moonlit night. My first thought was Cooper's. If there was such a thing as earning a drink, I think I accomplished that. I started in that direction and then a thought hit me. It was something that Sally Marsden had said to us.

She was extolling all of the traits of her daughter. One of them was her love of the garden. I remembered that Lois Winston's neighbor had said the same thing about Lois, about how hard she had worked in her garden that spring before her husband disappeared.

I turned and headed towards the back of the building to the vehicle pool. At the end of the day there were a few autos available. I signed one out and started the drive out to Lois' old house. It was after ten when I got there. I parked in front of her place and noticed no lights on in the house. There weren't many shining on the whole block. I got out of the vehicle and walked as quietly into the back yard as I could. The yard wasn't very big and only ran about thirty yards to the back perimeter. The edge of the property showed a lot of newer bushes that had done well since Lois planted them. In the left corner of the yard was a berm, the one that was Lois' pride and joy. At its highest point it was about four feet tall. It, too, was covered with plants, flowering bushes and some grasses. I walked towards it.

When I got to the berm I looked back at the house. There was a rear door that led into the house and another one that led to a cellar. There was maybe sixty feet between the cellar door and where I stood. I noticed the ground under me was still damp from the storm from the other day. The soil in the berm would be soft as well. I walked behind the berm and found a pretty good sized branch that had fallen off of a nearby oak. I pulled any remaining leaves off of it.

Back to the front of the berm I went. I walked up the first couple of feet, my shoes sinking in the soft earth. I slipped down to my knees. So much for this suit, I thought. Especially if I was wrong. Near the peak of the berm I began to dig. I heard a dog bark and I looked around. It was very dark and I couldn't see or hear any people. I kept digging. I had picked a spot between two small flowering bushes. I dug as fast as I could. My pants, my sleeves and my hands were covered in moist mud. I was down about two feet in the dirt. I was sweating and getting angry. I stood up.

"Goddamn it!" I said aloud. The dog barked in the dark, but he was far away. "How stupid am I?"

My temples were tightening and my stomach growled. I hadn't eaten since noon, but there was no way to go to Cooper's with mud all over me. I knelt back down and dug away with the branch and my hands. Sweat ran off my forehead into my eyes. I wiped at them with my sleeves. The dog barked again and I looked towards it. Nothing. I plunged the stick into the earth and I hit something hard. I thought it might be a rock. I dug my hand deep into the hole, still digging. I found what I had hit. I got my hand underneath and pulled up as hard as I could. Even in the dark, there was no mistaking. I held in my hand a human foot, fully dressed in a nice shoe. I had found the missing William Winston.

I returned the foot and shoe into its burial spot and covered up the hole as best that I could. Someone might see that someone or something had been digging in the morning, but it would be all over by then. I got back to the vehicle, got it started and headed towards my apartment. I knew that Lois had killed her husband. I also knew that he had beaten and abused her. She was a murderer. I felt sick about the whole thing, but I didn't see any way around it. I wondered what her plan was. One day, that body was likely to come uncovered. Where would she be then? No better than she was tonight.

• • •

It was very late and I was covered in mud as I trudged up the stairs. Hitting Lois in the face with her secret would not be easy. I'd have to take her into the precinct and someone would have to watch Freddie. What would happen to Freddie? Damn it, I thought. This was such a bullshit detail. I decided not to wake anyone. This could all wait until morning.

When I turned the key in my apartment door and turned on the light my plans changed. Right in my little living room sat Lois, tied to a chair, mouth gagged. She was able to turn to me and I could see the horror in her eyes. I grabbed a sharp kitchen knife and cut her free. When I released her arms she quickly threw them around me.

"Detective Moses, they've taken Freddie," she blurted out. Tears were already running out of her eyes.

"Slow down, Lois," I said. "Who took Freddie?"

"Men. Three men. They were all wearing hoods. They knocked on our door and grabbed me and then grabbed Freddie. They took me into your apartment and tied me up. I couldn't do anything."

My door had been locked when I left and when I came home. The only person that had another key was the landlord, Mr. Burkhart who lived on the first floor.

"They said they were taking Freddie to the Clark Street pier on the river," Lois said. "We've got to go."

She was dressed in her night clothes. "Go and change and meet me downstairs," I said. "I've got a vehicle."

She quickly left my apartment and went into hers. I walked down the stairs and one of my fears immediately hit me. Mr. Burkhart's door was slightly ajar. I pushed it open with my foot and stepped inside. I drew my gun and turned on the light. I didn't need the gun. Burkhart was sitting on a worn sofa, head back against the cushion. I stepped closer. A good part of his head and brain matter was on the wall behind him. A rather perfect hole was centered right between his eyes. Flash burns indicated the killer shot him at a very close range. I retreated and turned off the light and closed the door using my gun to draw it to me. Burkhart wasn't going anywhere. I could call this in later.

Lois came bounding down the stairs very quickly. I noticed she had the large revolver with her that she had used to chase my assailants away. I didn't know what we were getting into so who was I to object. She looked panicked, but took time to look at me in the hall light. "Detective Moses, where have you been tonight?"

Digging up your ex-husband didn't seem like the thing to say. "Let's just get going."

We ran out of the building and were quickly on Dearborn headed north towards the Chicago River. I knew the Clark Street pier very well. Gunter Krause and I had helped fish a body out of the river there. I hoped we didn't find another one tonight. During the whole ride to the pier, Lois didn't stop praying once. She might have been a husband killer, but she was a caring mom.

I took the bridge across the river and turned left towards Clark. The pier was right up against the street. I cut the lights on the auto as we got close. I cut the engine and parked behind some large containers. The thought of the dream of me killing Christian Hanson entered my head. Instead of the Hudson, maybe I shoot him and he falls into the Chicago River

"I'll go in first. Don't run ahead of me. This might be a trap to get me out here," I said.

"Okay," she said quietly.

"And don't go shooting that gun off, especially in my ear."

I drew my gun and moved cautiously out from behind the containers. The moon was still bright and the pier was well lit. At first glance, I saw nothing. Lois was right behind me. I could hear her sniffling. I moved ahead. There was a boat moored at the pier, but there was no activity on it. I got to the water's edge and we found Freddie. He was naked and tied to a mooring post. He, too, was gagged and his eyes were covered. Around his neck was tied a piece of paper.

"Oh my God," Lois yelled.

I freed Freddie and undid the gag and eye blinder. He fell into his mother's arms, whimpering like the small kid he was. I felt awful that he had been thrust into this. I took the note from around his neck and stepped into the only light that lit the pier.

It was a simple piece of white paper. The print was large and crude. A man had written it. The message was clear: NEXT TIME MOSES. Freddie had been taken as a warning, but by whom. It could have been Christian Hanson, but then another thought hit me. It could have been Jack Garfield's boys. There was no way of telling.

I walked back to Freddie and Lois. Other than having no clothes, he looked okay. He hadn't been bodily harmed. I took off my muddy jacket and draped it around him. We slowly walked back to my vehicle. Lois and Freddie sat in the back seat as we returned to our apartments. Freddie was still crying and Lois kept telling him things were going to be alright.

We got him upstairs and Lois quickly got him into his night clothes and laid him down in her room. I was sitting on a wooden kitchen chair when she came back out of her bedroom.

"This all has something to do with you," she said.

"I think it does," I said.

"What kind of men would use a small boy like this?"

I considered my two choices. The response was the same. "Ruthless men."

She crossed her arms and looked at me for a moment without

speaking. Maybe she thought she had found a place to live after burying her husband in her former back yard. My moving in had clouded that thought.

"I didn't answer the question that you asked me in the hallway, but since I have the feeling you may not want to live here anyway, I guess I can answer it now."

"What are you saying?"

"You asked me where I had been tonight, how I had gotten this mud all over me."

She looked concerned and was about to speak.

"Stop," I said. "When I asked what you missed about your house you told me a few things. Your neighbor told me you'd become an avid gardener this spring, right before your husband disappeared. You never mentioned to me that you missed your gardening. It made me wonder. Then it occurred to me that your gardening had only been done for a purpose. That nice little berm you built in your yard serves two functions. It's a nice spot for bushes and plants. It was also a nice spot to bury William."

Her arms dropped down to the side of her body. She looked guilty as charged. "You don't understand, Detective Moses. William was a drunk. He was seeing other women. Worst of all, he was beating me. I thought he might kill me. I had to do something."

"So you killed him?"

"I killed him."

"And you told Freddie this lie about him running off?"

"No, Detective Moses. You are wrong there. Freddie knew William was going to hurt me bad one day. He was very worried about me. I hit William over the head in cellar. I killed him, but Freddie helped me drag him into the yard and bury him."

My heart felt like it missed a beat.

"So what will you do, Detective Moses?"

I took a breath to calm myself. "I will call the detectives who have been looking for your husband and tell them where they can find the body. It will become damn clear who killed him and stuck him in that berm. There will be no life insurance payout, Lois. They don't give them to murderers."

"And Freddie and I."

Two wrongs never make a right the old axiom said. I knew at some point I might hate myself, but right now I hated men like William Winston more. "I am going to go to my apartment and get some sleep. It has been a long day." I got up and walked past her and crossed the hall to my own place. I dropped all of my sodden clothes at the foot of my bed and climbed under the sheets. It had been a long day. My head wasn't on the pillow for more than a few moments and I went to sleep.

*****

August 15th

I slept solidly that night and into the following morning. I woke up late and took my time getting ready and eating a little breakfast. I was in no rush. What was there to rush to? In less than two weeks I had seen a father kill his three children, a wife had killed her husband with help from her ten year old son and two thirteen year old girls had murdered three old women because they were bored. Then you could add in an investigation by a corrupt police captain and his men. Lastly, Christian Hanson was back out there. Normal people don't see this much evil in their lives. I wondered how normal I was.

Usually when I was under great stress my temples would ache terribly and my vision would become impaired. Today I felt nothing like that. If anything, I felt a little numb. I wasn't sure if that was an improvement.

I finished tying my tie and I put on my suit coat. I checked my pocket watch. It was ten past ten. I left my apartment and immediately noticed that the Winston's door was ajar. I thought something bad might have happened to them, but I knew better. I crossed the hall and entered their unit. Everything looked normal, but no one was home. I had one more thought. I walked into Lois' bedroom and checked her clothes bureau. It was completely empty. I crossed the hall to Freddie's small room and checked his dresser. There were no clothes in it either. I had given her a chance and she had taken it. I'm glad I didn't know where they were headed. It was better that way.

On the way out, I opened Burkhart's door, but he hadn't moved from his spot on the couch. Whoever took Freddie killed an innocent man. They went to great lengths to prove a point. They were dangerous men and these were dangerous times. There would be more danger ahead.

Once I got to the precinct, I made two phone calls. Both were made to Police Headquarters. They were simple calls. One told the desk sergeant where William Winston was buried. The second advised the same officer that Burkhart was dead in the apartment below mine with a bullet hole in his forehead. I hung up the phone and laughed. Burkhart had been killed in our district. I might be lucky enough to catch this murder. At least I knew what the motive was, to get at me.

There was a call to the Detective Division that I had a visitor downstairs. I looked at my watch. The arraignment for Patricia Farmer and Madeline Marsden had been set for one that afternoon. I didn't have to be there, but thought I might stop in. There wasn't much going on. At least not until this visitor showed up.

I walked down the stairs and there was a very tall, thin man, dressed in a tan suit, standing in front of the main desk. He had removed his hat and I could see thinning hair, combed straight back. He also wore glasses.

"Help you?" I said.

"Detective Moses?"

"That's me."

"Can we talk somewhere quiet?"

The man was reeking lawyer all the way. I motioned him into the meeting room on the first floor. I closed the door behind us. "What can I do for you?"

"My name is Bradley Luke. Yesterday evening you arrested Patricia Farmer and she will be charged with three murders this afternoon."

Luke had a pale face. It didn't look like he'd been in the sun all summer. "That all sounds about right."

"Well, Detective Moses, I am here to advise you that I have been retained by the Farmer family to represent Patricia going forward."

"Someone has to do it," I said, "but I would think there would be a lot easier clients to take on."

He angled his head and gave me a funny look. "Why would you say that?"

I laughed. "You have two girls who have admitted being at each scene and carrying out the acts that killed the three women. We have an eye witness placing them at one of the scenes. It doesn't seem too hard to figure out which way this case will go."

"So you say, Detective."

"Mr. Luke, I've got things to do so unless you tell me something to get me to stay, I've got to get moving along."

"Oh, I don't want to take up a lot of your time. It's just your version of things don't seem to mesh with Patricia's."

"How's that?"

"First, Patricia denies doing any of the bodily injury to any of the women. She says Madeline Marsden did all of that. Secondly, she says that you and your group of detectives intimidated her into saying some things that might not have been true."

I felt that tightening again. "Is this a joke?"

"No, Detective. I am afraid not. We don't think Patricia had a lot to do with the murders and we also think she told you some things because she was scared. Things that might not have been true."

"That's the most ridiculous thing that I have ever heard."

Bradley Luke smiled at me. "She's a thirteen year old girl. We will have to see how ridiculous it is at the trial."

He turned and walked out of the room, leaving me there to think about the outrageousness of his statements. My head began to throb and my vision got blurry. So much for feeling a little numb. I walked out of the door and headed for the exit. Desk Sergeant Coogan yelled something out to me, but I kept going. I had tried to watch my actions and had made it more than seven months, but none of the past days were making any sense. What was it the Wilfred Mannus had said to me in New York? There was no good, only different degrees of evil.

Was he right about that? I couldn't figure that out on my own.

When I walked into Soon Lee's the old man was busy making fresh noodles. The door jingled as I entered and he looked up to see me. He didn't look surprised that I was there. He actually looked like he expected me. He pointed me towards the stairs that led down to the opium den.

Until next time, The End

* 9 7 8 1 6 1 2 9 6 9 0 1 5 *